THE MARCH HARE
&
OTHER STORIES

Other books by the author:

Bean Aonair, Clódhanna Teo., 1974
Buicéad Poitín, Clódhanna Teo., 1978
An Lánúin, F.N.T., 1979
Na Déithe Luachmhara Deiridh, Clódhanna Teo., 1983
Lilí & Fraoch, Clódhanna Teo., 1983
Maigh Cuilinn: a Táisc & a Tuairisc, Cló Chonamara, 1986
Ar na Tamhnacha, Clódhanna Teo., 1987
Taomanna (caiséad & leabhrán), Cló Iar-Chonnachta, 1990
Gróga Cloch, Cló Iar-Chonnachta, 1990.
Íosla agus Scéalta Eile, Clódhanna Teo., 1992

THE MARCH HARE

&

Other Stories

Pádraic Breathnach

**Selected short stories
Translated from the Irish
by Gabriel Rosenstock**

Cló Iar-Chonnachta
Indreabhán
Conamara

First published 1994
© Cló Iar-Chonnachta 1994

ISBN 1 874700 03 6

Cover Artwork: Brian Bourke

Cover Design: Johan Hofstenge

Design: Cló Iar-Chonnachta

Cló Iar-Chonnachta receives financial assistance from
The Arts Council/An Chomhairle Ealaíon

Publisher: Có Iar-Chonnachta, Inverin, Connemara
    Phone: 091-93307   Fax: 091-93362
Printing: Clódóirí Lurgan, Inverin, Connemara
    Phone: 09193251/93157

Contents

(TRYST and A FRESHER are original stories in English by the author).

Pádraic Breathnach is a short story writer, essayist and novelist. His work has won many prizes, including **The Butler Literary Award** from the Irish-American Cultural Institute and **Duais Chuimhneacháin Sheáin Uí Éigeartaigh** from An tOireachtas. A native of Moycullen, Co. Galway, he lectures in Irish at Mary Immaculate College of Education, Limerick. He is married with three children.

Gabriel Rosenstock is Chairman of Poetry Ireland/Éigse Éireann. Member British Haiku Society, founder Haiku Society of Ireland, Hon. Life Member Irish Translators' Association, Member Irish Writers' Union. Author/translator of over 40 titles, he has translated into Irish the selected poems of Seamus Heaney, J.W. Hackett, Francisco X. Alarcón, Willem M. Roggemann, Georg Trakl, Georg Heym, Günter Grass and Peter Huchel. He has translated into English the stories and tales of Dara Ó Conaola, *Night Ructions*, and the novella *Sea Mission*. His first novella, Lacertidae, appeared in 1994.

Introduction

The Irish short story has carved its own unmistakable niche in world literature. Anthologists differ, as is their wont, but few would exclude such names as James Joyce, Seán O'Faoláin, Frank O'Connor, Mary Lavin, Elizabeth Bowen, Liam O'Flaherty, Aidan Higgins, Seán Mac Mathúna, William Trevor, Daniel Corkery, Julia O'Faolain, Bryan MacMahon, John McGahern, Anthony C. West, Seamus O'Kelly and Ben Kiely from the broad, official canon. How did all this come about? The short story in Ireland is said to have begun with George Moore's *The Untilled Field* (1903) and, to this day, is a vigorous art-form. *New Irish Writing*, once with *The Irish Press* (then exclusively in English) and now with *The Sunday Tribune*, offers annual awards, courtesy of Hennessy Cognac, and anthologists such as David Marcus and Dermot Bolger continue to bring vibrant prose in English to the attention of the literary public at home and abroad.

What is not well known abroad is that we have two literatures in Ireland, one in Irish, the other in English. Of the two, literature in Irish is immeasurably the older. The origins of the Irish short story go back, therefore, long before George Moore who, incidentally, wished his stories to be translated into Irish so that they might serve as a model for a new generation of writers in the neglected vernacular.

The origins of the Irish short story lie, in fact, in the elaborate tales of the *seanchaí*, the rich vein of storytelling which contributed to one of the great oral literatures of the world, a folk-art influenced by earlier classical forms in Irish – lyrical, heroic, topographical. Such distinguished practitioners of the art as Amhlaoibh Ó Loingsigh and Seán Ó Conaill were no mere purveyors of quaint, fire-side tales but supreme artists with hundreds of hours of spell-binding tale-weaving at their command. These stories may not have had all that subtle psychological insights of Chekhov, de Maupassant or Singer but they contained narrative, dramatic and linguistic trappings galore to enthral a discerning audience.

Irish-language writers, Máirtín Ó Cadhain, Pádraic Ó Conaire, the Ó Céilleachairs, the Mac Griannas, Pádraig Ua Maoileoin, Tomás Ó Criomhthain, Peadar Ó Laoire, An Seabhac and in our own day, Dara Ó Conaola, Joe Steve Ó Neachtain and Pádraic Breathnach himself, to name but a few, were all deeply coloured by the folk-imagination and by our 'Homeric' tradition of story telling.

Tradition is a boon. It can also be a burden. Breathnach is representative of a generation of writers in Irish bridging two worlds, sometimes wrestling between two cultures, two versions of what has made us what we are. He is, perhaps, most convincing when writing earthily about his own people, a people until recently victims of a terrifying marginalisation, aboriginals in their own homeland, ekeing out a grinding living on next to nothing, dispirited by the dole or by drudgery, destined, many of them, for emigration, bachelorhood, spinsterhood, celibacy, a people inhabiting a harsh physical landscape that echoed an emotional landscape, threatened with cultural alienation – at home or abroad – a people with a pagan attachment to place, however unbountiful.

Breathnach often writes about a loss of innocence with tribal as well as individual implications. He is good on vitriol, loneliness, blind hate, social awkwardness, guilt, self-doubt, the dreams of youth, rites of passage; he is glorious and unmatched in his depiction of decay, the decay of social, cultural and moral fabrics, of landscape and mind gone to seed.

I have tried to represent a cross-section of the author's styles and concerns in this selection and hoped for a balance between a rural world in its contrasting torpor and liveliness; glimpes of another rural world, less harsh than the western seaboard; seemingly homogeneous rural communities and those in transition; slices of urban life; idylls of youth; family life . . . I have chosen short pieces that are vignette-like and longer stories wherein a whole world unfolds, often in minute detail, complete with the energies of the animal, vegetable and mineral domains.

What cannot be conveyed here is the bold command of the Irish language, palpably evident in everything he writes. In my view Pádraic Breathnach is the most stunningly accomplished master of Connaught Irish we have seen since Máirtín Ó Cadhain and I am happy to introduce his gifts to a wider audience.

Gabriel Rosenstock,
Baile Átha Cliath 1994

The March Hare

As happened on so many other mornings it was his donkey's braying that woke Mikeen, a braying that sawed through the early morning air. He didn't know what time it was exactly. Mikeen didn't have a clock but he had an idea of the hour of the day from the pale watery light filtering through the curtains. He got out of bed immediately and went to the small window to catch a first glimpse of his pride and joy. And there he was, the faithful servant , as Mikeen knew he would be, standing proudly on the grey mound of granite rock on the airy hill, ears pricked, head over a ditch, taking in the countryside and the expanse of ocean.

"Praise God!" Mikeen cried. "Praise God!" Tears of joy and pride glinting in the corners of his eyes.

Mikeen dressed himself and crept stealthily out towards the hill. He didn't know if his mother heard him getting up, or lifting the door-bar, as he stole out. If she did she'd be calling him back. Her voice was in his ears.

"Mikeen! Mikeen! Come back in here, good boy!" She didn't like him going out that early, it was an unearthly hour to be up and no work calling to be done.

"Mikeen! Mikeen! Let you not be seen out there by yourself at such an early hour!"

But this was the hour that appealed to Mikeen. This was the time of day he liked best, the early dawn, when the human world was still in slumber. He liked the quiteness, the great peace, no one up but himself, the animals and the birds. He liked the gloomy colours of this hour; the sun not yet risen, but soon to rise as a magic, red ball.

The dew he liked; those shining drops on stem and leaf.

The fresh sounds of the country he liked, in this hallowed hushed hour. But he heard his mother's voice eternally. Telling him ceaselessly to be like all others, not to be a jackinapes, a holy show, a sight.

"Don't be an eedjit Mikeen!"

Pranksters mimicking her: "Don't be an eedjit Mikeen!"

He sat down on a rock. He glanced at his mother's window, wondering had she noticed yet. Many is the time he caught her, peeking out of the side of the curtain. The tiniest fraction of the curtain, so she wouldn't be noticed. She'd become bolder as soon as she sensed he had noticed her.

"That rock is wet, Mikeen!"

"You'll get your death of cold from that rock, Mikeen!"

"Your breakfast is ready, Mikeen!"

"Come in out of that, Mikeen!"

He'd come in after a while, when others were getting up. They'd be getting up earlier today, it being a Sunday. Off to Mass, the first Mass today as it was racing and regatta day.

The donkey was getting restless. He got restless around this time every morning. He flapped his ears. Wagged his tail. Kicked a bit. Shook his head. It wasn't horseflies or wasps that caused the uneasiness. They wouldn't be out in the early morning chill, not for a long while yet. Not horseflies, but exuberance, an exuberance heating the blood.

He decided to bray again. A deep, frothy braying from the bottom of his throat. For a while now, ever since he met the stranger, the young woman, the school-mistress from the city who was taping the sounds of the country for the city children, Mikeen had begun to differentiate between the various brayings of the ass. She was the cause of it, and if she hadn't inveigled his help he wouldn't have been around waiting for her. It was she who explained the braying to Mikeen.

"It has four parts to it," she said. "There's the first part, the second, the third part and the fourth."

In spite of shying away from her finery of dress and fine speech, he had to burst out laughing. He laughed and he laughed. He stopped in mid-laughter when he saw her staring at him and took hold of himself. He remembered he had often heard people describe his laughter, sniggering as they did so:

"An ugly laugh, Mikeen. The laugh of a laughing jackass!"

He became restless in the young woman's presence. Embarrassed. He asked himself did this young woman think the same. Did she think he had the laugh of a loon? He felt ill at ease. This is what happened to him in company. That's why he had no gumption in him, why he avoided society. He was afraid. Had she figured it out too?

"You've a lively laugh," she said. There wasn't the trace of malice in her.

"Yes," she said, eloquently, "the donkey's braying has four parts. The second and the fourth parts are the most noteworthy. The first part is little more than a sharp whine. The second part is hardly there at all as it's simply a massive inhalation in prepartion for the third; but it is the fourth phase which most interests us. This is the plaintive phraseology of phlegm, the roots of which are never fully expectorated. The hoarseness that gets to our hackles; a wild, shivering amorphous cry. The beauty is in the wild amorphousness. A terribly male thing!"

She was giving words to her own thoughts, according to Mikeen.

"There are intimations of immortality in the bray of an ass," she said. "A dreadful vibrational essence. The braying of a donkey is one of the most primeval of all sounds. A barbaric utterance!"

Mikeen grasped all she said. She was a wonderful

person, he thought, for a city person. A terrific woman. Sitting placidly beside him on the rock. Delighting in the day, in the countryside, in the company. Mikeen was glad she had arrived out of the blue. He was as contented as she.

"He brays all the time!" she said.

"He's young, you see!" said he.

Had he said too much? His uneasiness returned to haunt him. Did she understand him properly?

"I was thinking as much – I'd say he's feeling randy."

She understood. Did she? The donkey was letting down the doodle and taking the sun. A fly buzzed around the tip of the doodle and the donkey was trying to rid himself of it. No luck. Mikeen's mother was watching him. The anger boiled in him. The donkey spread his legs, hollowed his back, and the piss gushed from him. The young woman was not a bit put out.

"You're fond of your donkey," she said.

"I am that," he said.

"A proud animal," she said.

"That he is," he repiled.

He'd like some foals. Shining black, like the father. All the donkeys on the common had foals, or were in foal. A load of them over there by the lake. Some of them would be in season themselves before long.

"Do you like this place?" asked Mikeen.

"It's beautiful!" she said.

Mikeen wanted to ask her would she marry him. But in a flash she was standing up, a camera in her hand.

"I'd like to take a photo of you and the donkey!" she said.

It was just then that his mother came out the door and called him in.

"Say nothin' to strangers. Information is all they want. When they go home they'll be laughing at you."

Mikeen got up. He'd do what he did every day, at

dawn and at dusk. He'd go around, checking the stone walls of the plot. He'd replace any stone that had fallen, or secure one that looked like it might fall – or even if it didn't. And that was the chore ahead of him now. A chore his father had before him. They kept the walls in shape. Mikeen was proud of his stone walls. Strong walls these, sharp granite stone set in a way that the edifice couldn't collapse, no need to fetter, chain or spancel the donkey. A chain takes the jiss out of a donkey. Leaves him spiritless. That couldn't be said about Mikeen, son of Mike, that he'd let his donkey roam the townlands like a tinker's ass. The same couldn't be said about certain scatter-brains and their donkeys. Others let their donkeys roam, weekdays and Sundays. They cared not if dogs chased them to kingdom come. Some of them get into fierce heat and knock over a portion of their own walls. That's when the wigs would be on the green. They'd wake up in the dead of night with the power of longing. Away they'd go with a rogue of a stallion, clattering through the village, the stallion's doodle swinging like a pendulum.

Mikeen thought of the young woman and couldn't rid his mind of her. Whenever the sun burst from the clouds he'd think of her. When he sat on the rock he thought of her. When he heard his donkey braying he thought of her. Would she come back? How long more before she'd return? Everything about her was lovely: her refined voice, her sweeping hair, her attire, the fresh gorgeous face. Everything about her face was lovely: the lashes of jet, the dark eyes, the slender eyebrows, red lips, the curve of her nose, the prominent nostrils. What pleased him most about her was her attitude. She was interested in ordinary things: the birds of the air, the wind blowing, the rain. These were things he himself was interested in but he laughed or made sarcastic remarks about such matters. She had nothing but praise. His mother goading him not to whisper a word to strangers, for all they were interested in was wheedling information so that they could have a good laugh for themselves. The doctor telling him to socialise more. Society and work, said the doctor.

"He's a manic depressive. That's what causes the fits, he's alone too much. He should go out, circulate."

With whom? Where? Who were his friends? It was fine as long as there was work to do. Work kept people going. But where was the work since people stopped going to Caoch to cut turf? Everyone went out in those days to his own patch of bog. But the bogs had nothing to yield and the people burned gas or coal from the shop. People complained that the turf was an awful bother, it was slavery trying to get it dry and transporting it in creels, or in bags. And even when it was dry there was a power of work to be done: building the reek on the spreading ground, bringing the lorry to the harbour, making another reek if the boat to the island wasn't ready. Another reek on the far shore if there wasn't a contingent ready with donkeys in harness to bring the turf home. Another reek again at home, securing the fuel against the elements. Tedious, back-breaking work, and many were not sorry to see the end of the era but, as the doctor said, "It kept the body trim and the mind at ease."

Only the odd person harvested seaweed any more. And those that did were only gathering bundles for the iodine factory. You needed a rowing-boat for the likes of that, a luxury he or his people before him never possessed. You'd need a lot of help drawing in the seawed and where would he find that? Who'd go out with him? What did he know about collecting seaweed anyway? People would only burst their sides laughing if he brought it up. What kind of a bee has he in his bonnet, they'd ask.

"Take care now Mikeen!" they'd all be saying. The only seaweed he or his people ever gathered was a fertilizer.

That custom was gone too because nothing was being planted any more.

You could make a few shillings on the periwinkles and the shore was dotted with them but, as the proverb says, they're only food for hags. Nevertheless,the city gentry were eating them these days. But only school children would bother to harvest them. They'd fill bags of them and a boat would come once a week in the summer for the collection. The buyer was a Breton. He'd buy carrageen, dilisk, dulse if he could get it but the youngsters knew nothing of such and the old folks couldn't be bothered. They were all drawing the dole now. Moping about, trying to kill time, drifting into pubs, drinking stout, playing cards. He himself never drank a drop, never played cards. Since he left school he had little truck with others. In the top of the village he was isolated from other folk. He didn't bother with them, nor they with him. He avoided them. They avoided him. He was no great shakes.

Now, if he had a companion? Someone he could trust, go out with? There was lots you could do if you had a buddy. You could go to the races. A spin in a boat, or on the bus. If he had a buddy he wouldn't mind venturing abroad. He wouldn't mind going as far as the shop. It wouldn't be across the bog he'd go, or slyly over garden walls by cover of night, but out on the road like any man. If only he had a mate, what would he care about others? About crowds? What would he care for harbour, church or shop? He'd greet all and sundry and mix with them in a good mood. What harm in getting the wind up? Isn't that what life's all about? He'd get someone's wind up.

Why didn't he high-tail it out of the damn place when he still had his youth, when he had the chance, as so many others did, anyone with a bit of spunk in him. Live in society and not to be a lone goose?

"It's no more than a badger's den where they live!"

"A bog-road to a cave!"

"What road or boreen would they need? Sure they're no more than wild cats in a convent!"

Where would he go if he decided to get away from it all? What trade did he have? What sort of learning? Forty miles down the road and they wouldn't know what language he was speaking . . . what forty? Half that. The only language he knew.

"Poor old Mikeen, God love the mangy old whore!"

"Why doesn't he go out?"

"A terrible blackness of spirit comes over him."

"Fits I'd call it – pure frenzy!"

Mikeen felt some kind of an odd fit on the way. Another bout of the same. Would it be as bad as some of the worst? Would he be rudderless altogether? Would the mind slip the moorings? A fuzziness came into his head, the eyes swam in their sockets. He felt like braying, but all he could do was petition his Maker. Would he have to go off to the hospital again? He didn't like the 'oxpital'. He hated the sight of it. But the doctor said to his mother that he wasn't a danger to anyone else.

"No harm in him," he said.

Were it not for that he'd never be let home.

Mike went to the well of spring-water behind the rock to throw a cool splash over his head. The cold water often cured him before. It must be a holy well, he thought in his heart of hearts. It had nearly dried out but the yellow moss on the bottom was damp.

He pressed a clump of the moss to his forehead. He felt he was getting better. A thousand thanks to God! His heart no longer drummed, his breath came easier. The doctor said his own cure wasn't enough, too many drugs were dangerous.

"He should circulate . . ."

The races were on in Oileán Phréachán na gCearc, or

Kite Island as they were now calling it. Those who were taking part in the regatta had to take their boats out there. The big boat, the halfdecked boat, the hooker, the small *gleoiteog*, the larger *gleoiteog*, the *púcán* and the curragh. The larger sailing boats would pull the curraghs behind them. A lot of the young men would accompany the crews. Some of them would test their skill in throwing horse-shoes and the like and they'd want to be readying themselves in good time. A huge crowd of supporters would follow.

He hadn't been to the regatta in ages. Who'd bring him? Who would he ask for a ride? They'd be only jeering in the boat, making him out to be a simpleton. Even when the regatta was on in Oileán Ceo he didn't bother going. Viewed it from the top of the house is what he did. But he would be left with the island under his sway. He could spend the whole day on the hillock and not a soul to bother him. He went in home. His mother gave him a bite of breakfast. After breakfast he lay down on the bed.

His donkey's hoarse braying woke him again. He could tell from the antics that there was a mare about. The stallion moving from wall to wall. Head cocked, nose in the air. It was Paudeen Tom with his mare on a halter. "Go out to him, Mikeen!" his mother said. Paudeen was a companiable sort. Others would let their mares out at night, off searching for the doodle. They'd tear down a wall with the fierceness of their doodle-want. Bleary-eyed at morning, having spent the whole night looking for the mare (would you believe), and where was that bastard that had half the territory doodled and destroyed? Not a working donkey in the parish that the devil had left alone and it mightn't be all that harmful for the mare to be in foal "by a proper stallion", they'd complain.

But Paudeen Tommy was a gentle soul. Mike was grateful to him and not just because of the few pence he'd put in his fist. He was against taking any few pence at all because he was honoured by the visit. He felt as obliged to Paudeen as Paudeen did to him. Nothing could be better than Paudeen's yearly visit. He was a man again, going out into the garden with Paudeen. And he had every confidence in his stallion, that he would perform perfectly. The stallion trotted up to the mare, jigacting, farting. He covered her proudly.

"Isn't he mad for it," said Paudeen.

Mikeen was overjoyed with his stallion's dedication. It brought a twinkle to his eye.

"She'll have a fine sturdy foal after that!"

Mikeen felt himself growing in stature. He thought he was Finn Mac Cool.

"Bring her back tomorrow if she's still in heat!" he said.

"By all means. And the day after if needs be."

His stoop had vanished. Energy coursed through his limbs, his body purred vigorously.

It was a great day. It was permissable to be idle on a Sunday. The island would be his until evening. He could go out on the rise. He wouldn't mind a bit of company now. He wouldn't mind being at the regatta. Maybe the young woman would visit him? Or would she be at the regatta? He walked up and down the sand boreen. Up and down again, intently, it had become so sultry. So unearthily silent. He knew joy like never before in a long time. He plucked a blade of grass and chewed on it. He relaxed against a rock. The sea stretched out below him. Calm. A blue china plate. A haze webbing the harbour: sign of good weather. He counted the villages, starting form the right, that skirted the bay: Caorán an Phúca, Úirid, An Tamhnach Mór, Leithinis, Móinteach. He went on his hunkers. Inis Gé and Inse Bhán, those were islands totally deserted now. He remembered when they once had a community. Reclining full length on the ground he began to doze.

The surrounding countryside looked well, dappled with

flowers. Appealing colours. The shades of pasturage. Heavy granite boulders, flecked with lichen of many a hue. The brightness of rock projecting from the earth. Séamas Breathnach's little stony fields below. Patsy Mór's few patches. Seáinín Mháirt's couple of nooks. The perfect stone walls of Páidín Shéamais. The warm sun beating down on the whole lot of them. Mikeen often felt ennervated by them. He was their prisoner, he thought, and other times he saw their grandeur. Páidín Shéamais had a golden cock of hay, covered by a sheet, in a corner of the field. A well-constructed cock. Straw ropes keeping it in shape. Séamas Breathnach's little nook of oats was greenish still, not yet ready for reaping. Loosestrife amok in it. Séamas needed some straw to thatch his roof. He'd have to get rid of the loosestrife. It looked a mess on the thatched roofs. White butterflies and yellow ones dancing among the loosestrife. A grasshopper composed a tune. A newt sun-bathing. Close your mouth! Or the sailing boats will make no headway. But the boatmen were skilled, they only needed the slightest breath of air. It was a day for curraghs. Interest in boats had revived recently. The young people wanted to know more about them. A boat was an awful expense today. All the same, every boat that was rotting on the shore had been repaired. Boats were for pleasure now, and racing, such was the change that had come over the world.

Some seagulls paid a flying visit inland. They flew above him. It was like they were griping about something. When he was a boy he heard that seagulls had feet of gold, with little bells on them that tinkled. He never heard the tinkle but remembered his grandmother attesting to it.

Way below in the harbour a black bird was bathing in the water. It dived and came up again, spraying water on its head and down along its back. Pecking the water. Gruffly it ruffled its feathers. A shag, or a cormorant; it was not easy to say.

Mikeen stretched himself. He stood up. He had a good look around. The fandango would be in full swing now over in Kite Island. The rock-lifting, tug o' war, horse-shoe throwing. He had a stone himself that had a bit of weight in it. He lifted it over to the other end of the rise, where his mother wouldn't see him. Nervously he passed the stone from one hand to the next. It was heavy enough, a stone weight.

He emerged again and scanned the distance. Not a soul around. He took off his coat. He took the stone in his left hand and held it above his shoulder.
He began inticing himself:

"Good lad, Mike! Up ya boy-yo Mike!"

His mouth resembled that of a cod, sucking in air. He started throwing shapes as he had seen people doing.

"Good lad, Mikeen, you never lost it boy! Keep it up Mike, you're a powerful man!"

"You're the best in all Glionnán Mike, is what you are!"

And suddenly he spied his mother on the top of the rise. How long has she been there?

"Come on in now like a good boy!"

He was bothered. "How long are you there?"

"Good boy! I've a chunk of sweet cake!"

His anger subsided. His stoop returned. Hunched into himself. He grabbed his coat and followed her in. She sent him to bed after tea and he slept like a lamb. When he woke late in the evening a terrible loneliness gripped him. He knew the boats and the people had returned. They'd be down by the harbour preparing for the great *céilí*. There was always a *céilí* after the regatta. They'd all be merry, they'd have had plenty to drink at the races, and the laughter and talk would be flowing freely. They'd have more to drink down below. They'd be at it till the crack of day, dancing and cavorting.

He went out on the hillock again at dusk. The horizon was still bright but the brightness was waning. The sea looked dark and cold. Across the bay the coast was losing its delineation. But something else made him lonelier than all of that together. It was the music that was pulsing through the air from the harbour hall. The whole world was down there. On the spur of the moment he decided to join them. Off he went. Down through the stony fields. He wouldn't go into the hall. Not even as far as the door. He'd stay in the little field near the hall. He'd wait in the dark, by the stone wall, listening to the music and feasting his eyes on the revelry.

He wove his way furtively through shrubs and loosestrife, through reeds and marram. He walked on until he reached the little field, a spot near the hall. For a while all he did was peer through a chink in the wall. After a while he grew bolder and raised his head. He didn't think he'd be noticed. He did it again. He kept his head raised until he thought someone was looking at him. Someone had spotted him. Some rapscallion, play-acting outside the door, calling to one of his mates.

"Who's that stump over there behind the wall?" he said.

Mikeen raised his head to see if they were still looking.

"There he is again!"

Next time Mikeen raised his head a missile was aimed at him. It missed. Mikeen took a strange fit of playfulness. He raised his head. Would the lads aim correctly this time? They were sizing up the target. Mikeen thought they were having a bit of crack with him, that they were all in on this together, having a great time. But he had lost the thread of the story and now it would take a new twist.

The lads came closer to the wall and nothing would stop them hitting their target now. One missile after another.

"Who is it?"

The lads advanced to the wall and climbed up on it. Mikeen edged in to the wall, as close as possible, hoping not to be seen. He twisted and hunched himself into a ball. But they saw the black clump at their feet and started showering him with rubble-stones. He pretended not to be there, curled up like a hedgehog. They started to pour lemonade on him. They were choking themselves with laughter. Someone suggested to piss on him. One of them filled a bottle and poured it over him. Another pissed straight down on him. And another . . . and yet another. It was a terrible commotion.

A grown-up went across to the wall. He looked down. He ordered the lads to stop. Jumping over the wall he shoved his shoe under the 'hedgehog', dislodging it. Mikeen's hands and legs were locked together. His head was in his chest. When he was put on his back a torch was shone on his face and all could see the foolish grin on his twisted face. A pitiful dry grimace. A wall of faces looked down. He was a living wonder. A lad inserted a long, dry, grass-stalk into his ear, then up his nostril. He had it done before Paudeen Tommy could stop him.

"Mikeen, what are you doing here?" said Paudeen.

Mikeen uttered not a word, the silly grin remaining on his face.

"Go home, Mikeen, there's a good lad!" said Paudeen.

He told the lads to be away with themselves. Paudeen went off. Mikeen slunk away. He heard someone asking Paudeen, "who was that?" And he heard Paudeen reply: "Mikeen the March Hare."

The Easter Egg

She said she'd give me an Easter egg. Anne Madden
was her name, one of the Maddens, John the blacksmith's
daughter; her uncle was Peaitín Sheáin Pheadair. Anne
worked in the city, that place some distance down the road
that was full of shops and streets, bursting with people and
houses. That was where the bazaar was, whenever there
was a bazaar. You had to go through the city to get to the
races.

Our house was only an ass's roar from the Maddens.
Theirs was west of the corner on the road, on the right-hand
side, near the village; ours was east of the corner on the left-
hand side. If you stood outside our house you'd see the
Maddens' white house to the west, the east gable looking
back at you.

Anne worked in a shop. Her sister, Mary, also worked
in a shop. The shop in which Anne worked was better I'd
say.

"A big egg!" she said.

Bigger than a hen's egg, bigger than a duck-egg, as big
as a goose-egg or a swan's egg. A goose-egg was big. The
goose often layed outside, without a nest, laying the egg
neatly on the ground.

"It'll be in a box, wrapped in a bright paper and the box
will have a cover!"

A rectangular cardboard box, more or less like a shoe-
box. A man opening the shoe-box, uncovering the layer of
paper, revealing the shoes – except it wouldn't be shoes, but
an egg.

"A chocolate egg with a chicken inside!" she said.

A chocolate egg! A miracle! Magic! How could an egg

be made of chocolate? How could a chicken be inside it if a hen didn't hatch it? I found it difficult to imagine a chocolate egg. A yellow chicken inside. Her yellow feathers as soft as a primrose, little yellow beak, tiny dark eyes, weenchy little feet. Cracking the shell with her little beak, chirping all the while, letting the world know she was ready to emerge.

Anne used to cycle to work with Mary alongside her. They left early. Much earlier than when I left for school. It was said they often left before the crack of dawn. I'd like to do that. They went eastwards, passing our house; I'd go westwards and pass theirs. I'd bring a can of milk to them. They had a forge and not a cow or a hen to their name.

It was their mother who'd take the milk from me. You'd only see Anne and Mary on a Saturday evening or a Sunday morning. It was a Sunday morning when Anne promised me the chocolate egg.

"I'll have it for you by Easter," she said.

I was abashed.

I couldn't wait for Easter. Easter Sunday would be an egg-feast. Everyone at table with their own pile of eggs. I'd have a big chocolate egg with a yellow chicken inside – and all in a box. I'd open the box carefully. Placing the cover safely aside I'd unwrap the bright paper; they'd all be watching me but dare anyone lay a finger on the egg or box.

Easter came. I didn't get the egg that morning. Standing in the middle of the road I looked west. I spotted everything that moved. I began to feel let down and hurt.

I was worried that the chicken would die without air. She'd grow weak, fall over on her side in a faint. She'd die in the egg, the same as a 'glugar'.

Maggots creeping towards the egg, devouring the eyes of the chicken. Worms, insects, dung-beetles, the devil's coach-horse, all arriving to consume her neat little body. Her soft, yellow feathers would be mildew. I was devasted.

I never heard what happened to the egg. Never heard what happened to Anne or Mary either for a long time and when I did I was told they'd gone to America.

Cuckoo

A glass of brandy nestled in her hand. Jewels flashed in her eyes. A bloom shone from her whole face.

"Well I'll be – I'm pissed already," she said. "The second brandy not down yet and I'm on my ear."

She heaved a little sigh of contentment. Her lips opened in a smile.

"What the hell!" she declared. "This is powerful stuff, powerful stuff lad," to the young fellow behind the bar. She knew his father better. What a character he was. She would have preferred him to be there, they'd have a laugh, take the mickey. He'd be along soon. They'd all be along soon, the whole family. This greenhorn was too young for the job, though already in his teens.

"How's the oul' fella?" she said, mockingly. And when he'd be along she'd say "And how's your wee little withered stump of a tree?"

She'd have a few more brandies on top of these two before the day was out. There'll be some real flaming drinking yet between now and closing time, she thought. But no need to wake the dead yet. After this one she'd go easy. She'd go easy enough on this one even, because her mood was just right. That's all she wanted, to be in the right mood, to feel lively. She had a reputation to live up to. Lively without being foolish. That was it.

She wondered at the swiftness of the drink's effect on her. She was perfectly genial now. That proved she wasn't an alcoholic. A regular drinker consumes a lot. She only drank to set herself at ease. She had arrived early so that she'd be ready, at her ease. She'd take it nice and easy now for a while and then when the time was ripe a few more hefty ones.

"How's the oul' lady?"

"God save us."

Now if it was the father she might have some fun. She wouldn't be asking about his mother or granny but about his stick and would she whittle it for him. I'm telling you! But there'd be pleasant company before long and she'd have a few stiff ones. They all would.

She knew the small sprinkling of people that were gathered in the hotel but they were not the sort you'd intrude upon. They were seated at a little table in the corner, engrossed in their own lively chat, oblivious to the world around them. Not her type. The formality of their greeting annoyed her; but her own company would be along soon. What does she care about them, she thought in her own mind. One of them was the master of the hunt, however he came to be that, not being famous or titled or anything. He wasn't even a strong farmer. Full of himself all the same – may his pride fall out through his arse.

She brought her glass with her to the front door. She was anxious that the show begin. They'll be along now soon, in cars and lorries. That's the way it always is with a live hunt. The live hunt always starts in time. It must, but with the drag-hunt there's no such hurry. Spreading the scent depended on the master and on the officials. But as for that feckless fool there inside . . .

Anyway, it'll make a great day's hunting, with the weather cool. A little nippy, even, but no cutting wind. Not that it would be all plain sailing either for the horses.

"Well, you've arrived, you ould fox!"

She kissed him on the lips and allowed him give her a squeeze.

"How are you at all at all?"

She knew her lips were warm from the brandy. They went in together. A big steaming vessel stood on the counter and in it a huge ladle. The owner's daughter was ready by the vessel and beckoned with a faint smile. Bríd responded with her own sweet smile but cautioned her companion not to bother with the warm liquid.

"That's only swill," she whispered.

"Drink that stuff and you'll be wettin' your britches. Have a brandy. Just the one. You can have as much as you like later on. We'll turn night into morning yet."

She gave him a slap across the shoulders.

"You look very nice dressed like that," she said. The brandy brought a flame to his cheeks. It wasn't his usual drink but he was enjoying one now on her advice. She was his advisor. Indeed wasn't it she who had dressed him for the hunt.

"You look beautiful!" she said.

It was his first time wearing jodhpurs. The first time to wear a stock and a bright, gold, brooch-pin on which were engraved a horseshoe and the head of a horse.

"I've booked a good horse for you," she said. He hoped it would be a good safe horse as well as being a good jumper.

"You need do nothing but keep your two legs firmly on either side of him," she said. "Really just look after yourself, he'll do the rest."

He felt like saying that the type of horse he wanted was one that would look after rider and horse.

"When you're clearing a ditch just grab on to the neckband, or to the mane," she advised.

A number of vehicles had already gathered in the hotel yard and riders in their hunting gear rubbed shoulders at the bar-counter. Liam noticed that many of them had ladled into the big bowl. "They wouldn't touch the stuff if it weren't for the fact it's free. Some of them are so miserly they wouldn't stand the Almighty a drink," remarked Bríd.

She greeted people as they came in, kisses, embraces,

introducing them to Liam. Communal bursts of laughter, now and again a whisper in Liam's ear: "That one's a real bitch, watch out for that rogue!" Smiling kindly to the bitch. A toothy grin to the rogue.

"There's a sweet–tongued shrew!"

"Just look at this little dish will you!"

Acknowledging them with a friendly smile.

"How's it goin'? Long time no see!"

"Wouldn't trust that one. Is there a man in the room she hasn't laid? Slut."

"Haven't seen you in donkeys', dear!"

"A puck-goat if ever there was one," she whispered to Liam. "Do you know what I'd like to do, I'd like to make mince-meat of his balls and feed it to – as for yer wan! She'd get up on a turkey-cock, with or without a saddle!"

Bríd was in her element, drinking, nodding to people, chatting, laughing, taking the piss.

"This is Maxine!"

"Meet Yvette."

"Say hello to Tanya!"

"George this is – "

"Val this is – "

"I'm ok, I won't be riding. . ."

She'd have plenty time to shake off the effects of alcohol. She'd have a meal while the hunt was on, take forty winks and she'd be in top gear again, fresh and energetic by the time the hunt was over. She'd be ready for the hunter home from the hill. Since it was a drag-hunt she knew exactly where they'd finish up, the fields they'd ride through, the ditches they'd clear. She would be there, watching their return, standing in the hotel's daffodil-crowded sward.

"Come here and I'll introduce you to the master himself."

Gentle reminders to Liam not to drink too much, to take

it easy, as he'd be saddling up shortly.

"Sláinte!"

"You be careful now!"

"Thanks a lot."

"Good man!"

"You'll be bursting for a piss but if you're unable to unfasten your trousers devil bit of notice will be taken."

"What did I tell you? It's your day. And this is nothing. Wait till the fun starts tonight. That'll be something!" she promised, her hand forming a suggestive fist. She clinked her half-full glass against his empty one.

"I'll be looking out for you from the hotel sward and I'll see you coming and I'll see no one else but Liam," she said, a playful glint in her eyes.

She took his stock in her fingers and arranged it neatly for him. Checked the brooch-pin again. The front and the back of the jacket, blowing at the slightest dust or fluff.

She hoped Liam would prove well. That he'd be in his element clearing the ditches. He'd stay aboard. She didn't care about certain others or if their bones got a good rattling or even if they hit the deck, as their well-rounded posteriors would cushion them.

Liam would be fine. Who knows what might come of it? She had done him this favour.

"Don't forget the neckband and what it's for. Or a fistful of mane. It might be your first hunt but you've had plenty of practice."

*   *   *

"Come back here you! Pick that up! Where are you putting it?"

She attempted to smile, to soften her anger somewhat.

"Where do those shoes go?"

"Out, get out of there!"

'Dawn Avenue'. The name inscribed on a rectangular metal plate on the bare cement wall. She noticed it this morning. She was so used to seeing it as she passed by that, very often, it wouldn't register a thing. The name was in big green letters against a white background. She remembered when she got the job here, at first, how the name stood out, how it cheered her; it was a joy, an achievement to be working here.

How did such a narrow, dark, avenue acquire such a magical name? There might have been some sense to 'Sunset Avenue', as it stretched to the west though, if the truth be told, she never saw the sun sink down from here. The avenue was too confined, the buildings on either side too high to allow much sunlight fall on it. The buildings should all be razed to the ground, including the one she herself worked in, she thought. The avenue was plagued by cars. Cars coming down, cars going up, parked cars. Wars every morning between uppers, downers and the stationary. Bríd would brace herself for this at the mouth of the avenue.

"Here goes!" she'd groan. "Gotta get to the bottom of this!"

She would proceed down the avenue, as headstrong as any man, hooting the horn with the same impatience as the others, indicating 'fuck you too' as necessary. Slowly but surely making her way – come what may – and frig the begrudgers. She had to come this way, for many others it was only a shortcut. She had little sympathy for that lot. They should all be derouted.

Some of her colleagues were just as bad, going one way instead of the other. It should be a one-way. Not always knowing who it might be she often gave vent to her anger, surging boldly ahead, horn blaring, cursing with eyes, tongue and gesture, only to discover it was a colleague. Or she might be abused by one of them, for all she knew. And then the forgiving smiles. Some of her colleagues gave her the creeps. Their minds were dark, she thought, their talk no better than that of a hen, and they smiled at all and sundry as if they knew better. So ignorant, some of them, that they didn't realize they were ignorant. Some of the men stank, of body odour and unwashed clothes. You'd nearly choke. She often felt like training a hose on them, from crotch to underarm.

Is it any wonder she got headaches? Liam, what a misfortune he turned out to be, spunkless, an overgrown boy, a limp wimp. She thought she might be able to get his juices flowing but they'd all dried up. Maybe he was missing something, or maybe just odd, or imperfect, or not interested.

A parked car was blocking her way.

"You woeful bloody fool!" she exploded. She lost control of herself, pressing on the horn. When eventually the driver came and apologised she didn't respond, one way or the other.

She stopped the car and let out the pet dogs. If it weren't for the dogs she'd shrivel up with loneliness. Though her office block was separated from the others she was allowed to keep the dogs close to her in a small yard. She had few visitors during the day. As long as the dogs were there she was in no danger of being attacked. Whatever about the boxer, the Rhodesian Ridgeback wouldn't let her down. Not many knew how fierce the breed could be when roused. A male, which she kept for breeding. He earned a little bit on the side for her as there weren't that many of them in the country. He was the boy to ram it home! Watching him, you'd wonder at the diligence he showed performing his duty. A pity Liam couldn't learn from him. Two of them could kill a lion. That's what they were for: bringing lions to heel, capturing them, putting them in cages. Try engaging them with a stick, or a staff, and you'd soon learn enough about them – they'd tear you apart, limb by limb, and leave not a bone behind!

What a great pity, she lamented, that she wasn't married so that she could leave this lousy job. In her mind she screamed that half a man would do, as long as he was well-off; he had to be well-off. A fat wallet, the energy of her Rhodesian, such was the stallion that formed in her mind. Slaving away she was, at work that wouldn't tax the mind of a wren. Her father died early so she was deprived of a college education. She never said anything about her work to her friends, other than where she worked. She was athletic, with a good figure, and as far as they knew she was in top notch. It wasn't the riding alone that kept her in good trim: tennis, badminton, volleyball and basketball. How could they know what she was up to? How could they know what qualifications she had or hadn't got?

"Pick up those scraps of paper!"

"Dry that floor with a cloth!"

"Stop running!"

"Stop messing!"

"You're not wearing the proper shoes!"

"Chairs in a straight line!"

What? Tell her friends that it was she who swept the floor, opened the doors, sitting in a prefab. . .?

Getting older. No prospects. Once she thought – she was certain – that she'd be gone out of here long ago as somebody's wife, up in the world as Mrs. this or Mrs. that. Although she would keep her own name; and the children, if she had any, might also be called after her. Had she been too fussy? She did have men, of course, quite a few; many the storm in a man she abated. She knew how to do that. How to get those one-nighters up, their engines purring.

And after their exertions she'd enquire about their little stumps.

"Ah you stallion, how's the apparatus this blessed morning?"

"Lord above, what a powerful arse."

She would have her satisfaction with them too and sore they'd be from her mountings. Like donkeys in heat in the moist, hot nights. Mere lambs by morning. But she was no Amazon. They had their fun of her too. She was proud of how much she was able to give. She didn't demand too much. Nor was she too generous. Or too careful. All she had – all they had – was memories of lust.

But she wasn't over the top yet. Still in her prime. Life isn't all bad luck. There was still buckets of love-play left in her. Except for poor Liam. Feckin' eedjit. All dressed up and ready to go – and never coming. She gave a sour laugh. Clean-shaven Liam and his after-shave.

The rubbish bags. First thing every morning. It had to be done before the other workers arrived. She hated the black plastic bags. She always felt like kicking them, more than any man ever felt like kicking a ball.

Often as she announced that the rubbish had to be put into the bags tied, it was never done. It was she who ended up doing it, wearing those foul rubber gloves. Many is the time she filed a complaint, threatened strike, but to no avail. The bags in the boot of the car, out to the main gate. No work for a woman, demeaning, weight-lifting.

"Lord God deliver me from this drudgery," she pleaded. "Send me a man, as long as it's not Liam!"

Bad luck to them. You can't live with men, you can't live without them, she said to herself.

*   *   *

"Enjoy the soup?" she asked.

Another uneasy pause. She tried her damndest to think of something to say. No good. What's the use anyway? He

wasn't going to contribute much to the conversation.
Unless he started to talk about his health or some accident
or misfortune, or the weather. Closed in on himself. Noises
from his throat and nose, that's all; the odd twitch. Like an
animal. Did he notice the intervals of silence? Did he
notice anything? He was unlikely to come up with a subject
of conversation. A hum and a haw. No more.

"Wasn't too hot?"

"No."

"It's much nicer hot anyway."

"Much nicer."

"Nothing like hot soup, especially on a cold day. It's
quite cold today. But not bitterly so. It's often been
worse . . . this day last week, or was it . . .?"

She hoped he'd stop grunting.

"There was one day last week . . ."

"There was . . ."

Sufferin' Virgin!

"There was one day last week . . ."

"There was . . ."

"It was awfully cold . . ."

"It was . . ."

"Anyway, if felt very cold to me . . ."

"Yeah . . ."

If only the waiter would come with the meal she might
be able to think of something to say; praise the food, give
out about it, or something. At least they'd be eating. How
slow they were.

"Aren't they awfully slow!"

"They are . . ."

His grunting, yawning, sighing were driving her round
the bend. She had to put them out of her head or she would
crack up. They were like snufflings in an unfamiliar cowshed.

This place was not unfamiliar, though. It was here they
first met. He was there before her when she came in. In the

same quiet corner. He liked the nook. It wasn't her choice but that was the only table with a free chair. The room was full that day, clergy, middle-aged priests with a lonely look about them.

She scarcely noticed him at first, a country man sitting by himself in a black coat. It was the same coat. The exact same black coat. That first day, too, he puffed and grunted but she was not put out at the beginning. They were seated quite close to one another, and only they were alone. The waiters slow with the food. Now and again she would glance at him, sympathetically, indicating that they were being neglected, in all probability, because they were alone. Though he didn't look at her directly, or at least focus his eyes on her, she knew he was aware of her glances. She considered telling him that they should complain that they were being neglected. But he didn't seem to be in a complaining mood. He seemed to be resigned.

"Good day!" she said after a while.

He returned the greeting.

"Aren't they very slow!" she said.

"They are," says he.

"I think we should make a complaint," she said.

He said he wouldn't bother. His whole body became fidgety.

"Well I will!" she said and raised her right hand.

"Have you been here long before me?" she asked.

His sniffing and snorting didn't bother her then. His faint odour wasn't too offensive, the odour of cows, the smell of the country – it wasn't sweaty or genital. Genital odour was foul.

She asked who he was and what he did. He'd been to the mart across the street, selling calves. He had sold them all and had got a good price for them. Things had gone well, couldn't complain, if the product is good you get its true price; he had no cause to grumble. She said he was an easy-going man and that was nice. When she asked him who he was he said he was a Conneely. 'Ceannfhaolach – Wolfhead', she thought to herself, saying it was an interesting name. She glanced discreetly at his head and face. Of course, the resemblance would have faded over generations. And yet, she felt there was something wolfish about her dining companion. Of course, she thought, man is descended from an animal. He was once an animal. He still is an animal.

"What's your first name?" she asked.

"Patsy!" he said.

"Isn't that Patrick? I'm Bríd, Bríd Maher. Well, nice to meet you Patrick."

They shook hands. He said it was nice to meet her.

She was wondering should she leave.

"Nice place this," she said.

"It is," he said.

"It was a nice meal," she siad.

"It was," he said.

"It's nice when its nice," she said.

"It is," he said.

"Do you come here often?" she asked.

"On mart days, I suppose," he said.

She got up slowly, fidgeting with the chair. Then suddenly she asked him would he come for a drink. Where would he like to go? To the lounge or the bar? Either would do. He said he'd buy, and she let him. She found a comfortable chair, and relaxed. She'd take off her glasses shortly. Her scent was in his nostrils.

She concentrated her whole attention on him. She would show him that he was the only man in the room. She asked him a lot of questions, she listened carefully to him, she praised him. She would show him how interesting he was. She convinced herself that he was capable of conversation, given the right circumstances. She persuaded him to allow her to buy the next drink, though she allowed him to go to the counter.

"Women!" she said. "They want to be independent!" She smiled beguilingly at him. It was only proper, she said, that they should pay their own way. She finished her drink and made as if to leave. She'd be wise and not spend too much time with him at this juncture. She knew, she said, that he wouldn't hold it against her if she left, that she had some chores to be done. He began to hurry too.

"I hope you're not rushing because of me," she said. She preceded him as far as the reception. She turned around at the door.

"I have to say Patrick that I greatly enjoyed your company. Sure we might meet again sometime. Good luck now Patrick and God reward you!"

She drove away, feeling good in herself. Little flutterings of satisfaction, anticipation and pleasure coursed through her body. After a few miles she decided to stop for a coffee and collect her thoughts. So what if he was only an old geezer, it might come to good. Who knows? Who knows what good might come out of it? The town had a mart every week. She'd bide her time for a month. No, she wouldn't – she'd meet him again in a week and maybe then lie low for a month.

She strolled into the yard of the mart, high boots on her with heels that weren't too high, her hair tied back in a bun. She was wearing a heavy woollen pullover and corduroy britches that disappeared into her boots. She walked cautiously, glancing here and there, looking at the men all around her. She was hoping he'd be there. Would she recognise him?

"Do you know a Patrick – Patsy – Conneelly from Muine, if you know him is he here today?" she asked.

"I know him well! Look at him over there!"

She faced in the direction she was told. Was it he? Could it be a brother or an uncle? He seemed shorter, she thought, smaller and older.

"Hi," she said. "I don't know do you know me at all," she said.

"Oh I do," he said.

"I'm Bríd," she said. "We met in the hotel."

"How are you doin'?" he said.

"We had a drink together, if you remember," she said.

"Oh I remember!" he said.

"Well, how have you been Patrick?" she said. "How's the mart today? Are the prices good? You're happy. Isn't it a nice day?"

He was shy, she thought. Maybe it'd be better to call him Patsy.

"How's business Patsy?"

Did he have a brother, a sister? Was his mother still alive? What kind of a home did he have? What class of a farm? Had he sheep, horses or pigs? Did he have a chicken-run, ducks or geese? What kind of outhouses? Was it an old house he had, a big two-storey house or a bungalo? What kind of a yard did it have, or haggard?

"Everything fine then Patsy? I'm glad."

She smiled happily in her heart when she thought of her capers.

She had told him she liked country ways, that she was a countrywoman herself at heart, that the happiest years of her life were spent in the country. She tried to be as good-natured and as placid as she could manage. She suddenly said that they should meet again sometime and have a drink together.

"I think we should make an appointment," she said capriciously. "Let's arrange the day and time," she said. She indicated that it was a date by taking out a small diary from her bag and marking the day, the time and the place.

"Don't you let me down now Patsy Conneely!" she said solemnly, reminding him again of the appointed time and place. She turned on her heel and waved farewell and walked carefully out of the mart.

*   *   *

Piece by piece Bríd was gathering the information she needed. Patsy was living on his own. His mother was dead and he had no brothers or sisters, at home or away. Nor sheep, because they were too bothersome. Nor pigs. Sheep were always getting entangled in bushes and briars, or were full of fluke in warm weather. As for pigs, there was no money in them unless you had a legion of them. They were forever causing damage and blue murder. And the day of the work-horse was long gone. Only the big buckos had them, for riding. As for hens, ducks, geese or turkeys, only women were able to look after them properly. Like pigs, ducks and geese ruin land with their poisonous mess. If you hadn't a constant water supply they weren't worth keeping. Hens weren't too bad, but for their habit of uprooting filth. He used to keep them before the fox got them all. He never bothered getting a new clutch. A woman was needed.

At long last he brought Bríd to see the property. She had often wished to visit it secretly. They travelled many a side-road and byroad. It was the heart of the country. More like the heart of the jungle: hedges and bushes sloping down wildly on both sides of the little roads. The roads themselves spattered with mud and manure. The remoteness of it all began to fill her with sadness and fright.

Patsy's place was much the same: a huge, rambling house, three stories high. Not a curtain to a window. Staring blankly at a haggard full of muck. A dark, spiritless mansion. The window frames half rotten. Likewise the front door. A dirty grey, the walls, the sluices on top broken, leaking, as were the pipes. Flecked with lichen: sluices and walls. The slated roof so high up you couldn't see much of the top of the house.

The house was a nightmare. Rot, dampness, dry rot, woodworm. Old bags, old coats, old shoes, knicknacks and rags all over the place. All the rooms, the kitchen, the porches, were a mess.

The outhouses were as bad: bundles of rubbish, hay everywhere. Old vehicles, old machinery, old cowboxes and horseboxes in the grounds surrounding the house.

What most offended Bríd was the entrance to the house and the road to the back. The wild trees hanging over the road, the hedges, the briars, the bushes; the banks of earth and borage most disturbed her. They would have to be trimmed and cut. As to the house itself, the solution was simple: knock it down. The house, the outhouses, the stables – they'd all have to go. Patsy had plenty money for the job, though he didn't show it, plenty land and livestock, plenty state grants. Not spending a penny. She'd put his wealth to use soon enough.

Bríd had visions. She saw what could be accomplished. A great tract of land, good fertile land, nothing wrong with it but gone a bit wild. It wouldn't be that way for long more. Fences would be taken down, ditches raised, drains cleared, swamps and slushy places put in order. She wasn't going to have a mud-farm, with the mud in on top of her. Not for her. She'd put some shape on things. Blast those rocks to the heavens. She'd spend her husband's good money to purpose. The bogland would yet be fallow land, where once was bush and briar would ring out with the praise of fine grass. Was the era of the horse over? The era of the cob. But she would have hunters and thoroughbreds munching the green grass . . .

He was smacking his lips. Doing his best with his

tongue and his teeth.

"Did you like your meal?" says she.

"I did," says he.

"Was the beef tender enough?" says she.

"It was!" says he.

"Wasn't undercooked?" says she.

"Was not," says he.

She wanted to tell him to stop smacking his lips, that he was like a cow. Smacking, snuffling, hiccupping, grunting.

"Have you a bit of meat stuck in your teeth?" she said.

She asked the waiter for a tooth-pick. She wanted to ask him did he need a handkerchief as well.

"Would you like a drink of water?" she asked.

She looked at him. She had no desire for him. None at all. But he was a man, a man of substance. She desired his substance. She also desired an heir, though not necessarily with this man. Let this man lie with her! Go to the altar with him! He'd be well washed, scrubbed, scoured and togged out. After the marriage she'd take the helm. One bout of sex, maybe, if he had it in him. She'd do all she could to help him, rub him, squeeze him, fondle and caress his balls and his member, so that he'd do his duty properly. She'd put up with his puffing and panting, his slobbering, she'd close her eyes and ears to all that and would pray all along that his labours would pay fruit. She'd drain the last drop from him. That was it then, her egg boiled. He'd be satisfied. She'd raise the child well. She'd be in full charge. With the egg, her nest and her nestling. She'd be a force with which to be reckoned.

She would demand her ways. It was for his good. She'd deal with him kindly. He could go off to the marts, his cows and his calves, but let him not try, as many of his kind did before, to dispossess her. If he did it would be he that would be dispossessed. He'd be the one to lose all. But if he treated her with kindness and did what was right, he had nothing to fear.

Zazzi

There's a big shop at the end of the street, by the crossroads, where all sorts of things are in demand. People come from far and near for loaves of bread, croissants, pizzas, quiches; they come for jam, for flowers, for honey. Newspapers are purchased there, apples, pears, plums. It has a post office, too, where stamps can be bought, of course, as well as raffle and lotto tickets.

It was here he first laid eyes on her, her back to him in the queue. There wasn't much else he noticed, other than that she was there, the small woman ahead of him in the queue. He knew she was no longer a girl, that she had reached the peak of her growth and wouldn't grow any taller. He was able to look over her head. She was small, but not entirely lacking in stature, as he was tall. He liked small women, as long as they weren't puny.

He took notice of her hair. Not a close examination, just the odd look – an easy task given her moderate height. He didn't wish to be noticed, observing her. Her face, he wanted to see her face. Difficult, she remained so still. He'd have a better chance in a while, when she would ask for whatever it was she wanted. Often the face would fail. Often not match the image. It often disappointed, stifled further interest or caused consternation.

His interest was growing. He was hoping more and more that she'd be right, that he had put the proper head on her, befitting her body. He liked the hair, from the back, the shoulders, the body shape. He began to examine her lower quarters, his eyes darting to her legs. He could just barely see the hollow behind her knee. He saw her calves. What kind of shoes were those? Hard to see them properly. She had a peculiar fragrance. A fragrance that could hardly be called that, hardly there at all, which only hounded him the more to test it in his nostrils.

Later she was in the shop, basket on arm, strolling by the shelves. He watched her scrutinizing the goods; examining the broccoli; taking a bunch in her hand, looking at it closely. Broccoli was a vegetable he never bothered with until now. Ordinary vegetables, turnips, cabbage, carrots, these he knew. But a lot of new vegetables had come on the market in recent years. He never bothered with spinach or leeks. Women mostly bought the new vegetables. Radish, pepper, garlic. Yellow peppers had been around for a while now. He'd seen the women putting them to their nose. Testing them that way. He liked the smell of turnips a lot.

He noticed her breaking the broccoli stem and discarding it in a bin before weighing the vegetable. That took a bit of nerve, he thought; the owner wouldn't be too pleased if he saw that type of carry-on. He wasn't around to see, but his assistants were. Had nobody seen her but himself? She was so matter of fact about it, as if she didn't care. It wasn't a bit anarchic.

"Excuse me, Madam!"

"What's up?"

"One buys the stem with the head!"

"Well one shouldn't!"

No assistant would have the gall to approach a woman of her self-possession. No boss would have the nerve. He'd order stemless broccoli from now on.

He studied her. Studied her gait. He liked the way she moved. The way she purchased her goods, the walk of her. Who is she? From where? What family? How odd he hadn't come across her before. A blow-in? He wanted to talk to her, small talk, to say he liked the way she took the extra weight off the broccoli, it would be stemless from now on and meat trimmed of extra fat.

"Who might you be?"

"Where are you from?"

"Do you have a name?"

"A job?"

He didn't ask these questions. He didn't talk to her about the broccoli. He didn't advise her on the best way of judging a turnip. He didn't say a word to her. All he did was to take her in. He took her in and felt what it was like.

He noticed the way she spoke when she greeted the assistants at the cash register. An agreeable voice. Her voice reflected good upbringing and confidence. She was a happy person. Her face reflected that happiness; her complexion shone with it. How smooth the skin on her face – a baby's bottom taking the sun and air.

"Hello there!"

"How are you?"

Her hair didn't reach her shoulders. It wasn't permitted to do so. Styled and brushed back well from her forehead, only covering the tip of the ear, her two lobes studded. Her neck was bare and visible, too, the initial sloping of her breast. Her face, her neck and bosom, her every part matching the proportions of her body. Of particular interest were those soft-brown eyes, the perfect eyebrows, the fairy-brushes that were her eyelashes. The vaguest hint of a snub nose. A sensuous mouth.

She was wearing a well-cut brown coat, browner than her hair, that stretched almost to her knees, fronted with large buttons. The shoulders padded. The sleeves covering her wrists; her hands were small, her fingernails longish, in their own bright, natural, pink. Both her wrists sported bracelets and she also wore rings, but her marriage finger was bare. Her brown shoes matched the colour of her coat. She stood as straight as a rush.

"A sophisticated young lady," thought Richard.

"A fine little filly!" he said to himself.

He longed to know her name. Elaine, Sophie, Sally or Corrainne? Sue, Suzanne, Jenny? Zöe, Rose, Breda or Mazarella? Máire, Maxine, Muireann, Mairéad? Mandy, Tracey, Lucy, Vicky? Basta, Ciba, Sufi, Zanussi? She walked out of the shop, looking straight ahead, he already regretting he hadn't made contact with her.

Who was she? Where did she live? A voice in him said she was someone special, goading him to believe they were fated for one another. People meet in unpremeditated ways. He made himself some dinner, his mind swarming with thoughts. She had impressed herself upon him in a mysterious way.

"I have seen a very special woman!" he said to himself.

"The woman of my life," he said.

He would see her again. If it meant searching the wide world.

He saw her, alone, on the street. Walking towards the shop. Would she go in? He followed her, inconspicuously. She walked past the shop. Now she was on the circular country road. Was she going for a stroll?

He continued to track her. Staying well behind. She proceeded at an even pace, looking ahead all the time. It didn't appear that she was only out for a stroll. Returning from work, maybe? A footpath ran the length of the road. She stayed on the footpath. Very few people were out walking today. Cars whizzed by in both directions. He had an idea that she lived out here, somewhere. But where exactly? He began to notice the houses, many of them new. Fine houses. He quickened his pace. What would he do if she turned back and started walking towards him? He couldn't just turn as well. That would be too obvious. He'd have to meet her head on. He hadn't his best clothes. Would he be impervious? Would she? He would look at her and would smile – if she were looking at him, and about to smile. He would greet her and maybe even start up a conversation.

She had reached the roundabout. Which way would she go now? She did something he hadn't expected: she went up on the rise, a grassy bank with a little cement path. He hadn't noticed that path before, even though it had two protective railings, as you'd see outside a school, at its entrance. She stooped and went through the railings. He never knew there was a house beyond that rise but now could see the top of the roof as plain as day.

*   *   *

The following evening he decided to go for another walk. He intended to climb the rise in the hope of meeting her. This time he walked differently: he was much more aware, of himself and his surroundings. This circular road was hers, this countryside hers. He noticed the whiteness of the path like never before. It was white because it was new. Its surface was rough, purposely, it seemed, to retain a grip in frosty weather. He perceived its length and breadth, and the lines in it, allowing it to expand in sultry weather. He liked the verge-stones.

The earth embankments on the side were to keep tinkers away. Nevertheless some families had managed to ensconce themselves in the gaps. The earthen mounds had sprouted grass, weeds and wild flowers. He began to name them. He was good at that sort of thing. He didn't know had she noticed? Had she any interest in nature? The fields surrounding her house were brimming with daisies, dandelions and creeping buttercups. The odd cow, the odd calf, a heifer or two, or a bullock. In one of the fields, all alone, stood a white horse, dawdling. He took it for an old pet, once ridden by a daughter or a son.

He climbed the rise. He saw the house. It had its own

road to the roundabout, as well as the little path. A strong odour of honey assailed his nostrils. Was it from a bee-hive? Or a lime tree? Whatever it was, its scent impregnated the air. A large, well-kept green on each side of the house and another at the front. Were the daffodils hers? The flower beds? Hers the flowering trees? The lilies, the laburnums, the cherry trees? Were the magnolia bushes hers? The Berberis hedge, *Berberis Darwinii*? Did those Friesian calves out in the field belong to her, to her people? Whose the horses? He hoped they were hers. He walked away, but he would be back again.

"Today I walked up to your rise. Saw your house. Good view of the countryside from up there."

"You've really got a hold of me," he wrote.

In some ways he was in her thrall, in other ways she had bestowed freedom on him. As though she had given him wings, had given him flight and the wherewithall to see the land.

"Today again I walked up your rise . . ." he wrote.

Maybe sometime in the future, were they ever to be together, sharing their love, he would show her what he had written . . . He wished it might be so. That they would some day sit or lie together on the gentle grass and he would weave her a daisy chain, a chain of primroses, a cowslip chain. They would walk the fields and groves together, the meadows, the glens and the woods.

"I often pass your house. I pass it by day and under the shelter of night. I long to catch a glimpse of you. Every time I see you, giddy ripplings make my heart feel strange, every time I think of you. Fresh visions burgeon and new desires, each time. I peer at your house, at the front garden and the flowers that adorn it and I ask myself where are you, what are you doing, where in the house are you now, which room is yours? Who owns the Starlet car?"

Some day he would show her his thesis. He believed that day would surely come.

"There's an old deserted house near yours, almost hidden by the grove of lofty trees. Its called Thorny Meadow House. See how well I have done my research! The avenue leading to it is scarred with wheel tracks, some large enough to swim in or to fish-farm. Weeds abound on either side. Coltsfoot is plentiful. There was a time, I gather, when the avenue was graced with smooth stones from the beach. A farmer owns it now. When you were young, did you go there to play? Did you play among the tall trees there, did you climb them? Did you ever 'rawk' apples form the orchard there? The orchards high walls are still standing."

"I walked the avenue of that old house the other day, thinking of you, wondering what you were like as a child. The house has gone into decline since, little more than a ruin, closed up except for the outhouses where they keep calves. Most of the windows are blocks of concrete now. It's a terribly lonely place. It would frighten you even by day. Crows were making a din and other birds flying in and out. It was chilling, the noise they made. The place is hollow, spectral. I thought of you. I left."

"In the surrounding fields cows were lying down, mothers chewing the cud, their calves beside them, each one content under the scorching sun. And my thoughts turned to you. Used you walk these fields? Used you walk as far as the canal and the winding river beyond? Do you still do it or are you like all young women, afraid of the 'bull'?"

*   *   *

After the rain the sun sparkled. It became exceedingly warm. He walked on up the road and climbed the rise. The countryside was in bloom. His eyes rejoiced at all the variety of flowers. New flowers had bloomed. Laughing brighteye had transformed the scenery. New flowers on all sides, of varying colours, shapes and sizes. Such happy faces, each one with its own pearly drop of rain. Each face, each eyebrow, each shining eye looked up peering, peeping, laughing. They winked at him. They giggled, danced, they sang a ditty. He wanted to present her with an armful of them. Invite her out. To ask her to gaze upon them, to fondle them, to inhale their nectar in her nostrils. Currents of air flowed all around him, soaked in fragrance. His heart began to race. The sunrays tasted sweet. They penetrated through his rib-cage and reached his heart, wrapping him in a cloak of ecstasy. The contented call of the cuckoo resounded in his ears.

"You're a young school mistress. I found out the other day! You teach junior infants. Such fortunate beings! You walk home from school. I know your name. There are others teaching at the school, young buckos some of them. Let them not steal you from me!"

*   *   *

He took a shower. The warm water streamed over him. He dried himself in front of the mirror. He considered himself, thinking of her. "You're a young man, tall, athletic, handsome, with a sanguine nature, looking for a sympathetic schoolmistress interested in having a spanking good time. Marriage essential. Box No. ...."

He was having an erection. He observed it, becoming engorged. A pulsating crow-bar with a halo of tension surrounding it. I'm a fine energetic lad, he said to himself, twenty five years of age, six foot tall with a good job, active at sports, interested in travel, music and drink, own my own flashy car, my own flat, I'm a damn good cook. In a word, I'm a helluva handsome hunk – yours for the asking!

He got into bed. He began to kiss her and fondle her. He embraced her, squeezed her. Kneaded her flesh. Layed her on the flat of her back and mounted her. Her backside was firm, her breasts full, her nipples erect. Her cunt dissolving as he plunged into her, thrusting to her innermost limits. Her pussy gripped him like it would never let him go.

He withdrew slightly from her only to fill her once more with greater fervour, and passion. Greedily he explored her, kissing her forever, embracing her again and again, squeezing. Exploring deeper and deeper inside.

He lifted her legs and she fastened them around him and drew him to her. She lifted them to his shoulders and he was noosed – oh the silkiness of her thighs and the open nest as his member harried her once again and it was like his prick was a hungry orphan being suckled. Balls and all he'd shove into her! She was everything now, nothing existed but her crazy cunt awash with juices. He sunk his fangs into her shoulder as his seed exploded, cascading through his shaft inside her. He lay sprawled on her, panting.

Her hands were rope-like around his flaming body. Sweat oozed from every pore and turned to beads, coursing down his limbs. They dropped on her.

"You're perspiring," she said with a gentle smile.

He looked at her face and gave her a little peck. Her face had the colour and texture of pink roses.

"You're drowned in sweat," she said.

She asked him for a tissue. The sheets were drenched.

He saw her the following day, driving from her house in the Starlet to the roundabout. Dressed in summer wear. She raised her hand to him in a greeting. It had a glove on it. The hand he loved.

A Darling Priest

Would they go to the half-seven evening Mass or wait until morning? They usually went to the Saturday Mass, unless Ian was serving on a Sunday. She liked to have Sundays free, especially the mornings; but she felt tired and indolent this evening. They'd wait, unless Ian was serving. Where did that list go to? It was always hanging in the kitchen, but it wasn't there now. Who would have taken it? Did it fall off?

She opened the kitchen door and gave Ian a shout. She heard the music streaming down from his bedroom, if you could call it music. He spent too much time playing that music instead of practising on the piano. It occurred to her again that he'd been remiss in this regard and she suddenly felt fussed and angry about the whole business. She regretted that they were unable to sell the old stereo. But she had to admit that he was putting it to good use, or to some use. As for the new stereo, Ian was the only one who used it. When you think of all the records they had bought! It would never be used except for Ian and it was reluctantly enough that he had been given permission. Hadn't he his own, they told him. But the new one has a radio, he protested, and lots more beside. He was warned to be careful. Though they knew in their hearts that Ian wouldn't be the one to break it if it ever broke and, even if he did, that he'd be able to put it together again. Ian had the knowledge, that much had to be said of him. Young people were wonderful in this way, masters of the 'technology', a word that always took her aback. She herself knew nothing about it, no more than her husband.

"Turn off that confounded machine," she shouted up to him, impatiently.

"Is it deaf you are?" she roared.

She went to the bottom of the stairs and called out loudly again. Some song by Michael Jackson or George Michael or some such bostoon and he taking no notice at all of her. Or that numbskull Madonna. "Papa, don't preach!" That red-lipped, shameless hussy gave her the creeps. Her own son listening to that one, watching the lecherous wanton. U2 weren't all that bad. "I still haven't found what I'm looking for."

"And isn't it a pity for you that you haven't!" But at least they could sing and had some sort of music.

Def Lepard, A-HA Wet, Wet, Wet: "Wishing I was lucky." Such names, such songs. Tripe! The whole shootin' gallery of them – groups and songs alike – a wren's fart. A song today, gone tomorrow. That's not music – its raucous noise. Shouting! Meaningless yelping. Inane lyrics. And people say it keeps a person young.

He was playing a song by Bros: "When will I be famous?" She had to admit that the song agreed with his outlook. All he thought of was fame and riches. People asked her about Ian: what's he going to do when he grows up?

"A lot," she'd say.

"Going to be a movie star," he'd say.

That's what he was going to be. To hell with the Leaving Cert, he'd pack off to America, to Hollywood. She heard him singing in tune with the cassette. Lying on his back on the bed, no doubt, soaking in the gist of the song, in a world of dreams. She nearly had a fit realizing she'd have to go all the way up the stairs.

She took no heed of the notice on his door and barged her way through. He sat up with fright. A sudden flush came to his cheeks.

"Why didn't you knock?"

"Look," she said, "will you have a bit of sense!"

"You have a bit of sense!" he said back to her.

"Ian!" she pronounced, solemnly.

"Well how would you like it if I came into your room without knocking?" he retorted.

"Not the same thing!" she said, firmly.

"Well I think it is," he replied.

"Well I don't care what you think!" she said.

'RULES OF THIS ROOM!' Up on the door. In stark bold capitals ordering: not to enter, knock first, and all that. I'm busy, I'm asleep, I'm listening to my stereo, in communication with a being from Mars, dismantling a bomb and much more besides. Such rubbish! Codology! The ravings of youth! Soon he'll think he owns the house. And it didn't help matters when he said that Daddy always knocks. He can do what he likes, she said. It didn't matter one way or the other to her. If he was a bit more like her there wouldn't be half as much trouble, she thought.

His brand new T-shirt similarly defiled with scribblings. Duran Duran emblazoned in durable ink. All his T-shirts smeared with names of pop-groups and slogans. Pictures drawn on them, designs and symbols. All his clothing ruined. She wouldn't mind if he had kept one article intact for Sunday. His father's fault again. No spine. If he had he wouldn't put up with this. She told him so, she said he had no back bone. The same business again with hair styles, buying shoes, coats, jackets. "Leave it to himself!" That's what his father said. Why would she leave it to himself, to Ian, to a mere child? She didn't see eye to eye with her husband. In time to come they would lose all control over Ian.

The walls of the room reflected his taste in T-shirt creations. Not a square inch able to breathe with all the pop-posters and the stars' paraphernalia – guitars, bikes, flashy cars; those reedy women on the bonnets. Half-naked, sun-soaked creatures with their outsize sunglasses in gaudy colours, nothing on them but G-String bikinis, or (suffering Jesus) garters. Gross! What gear? The feminists were right, about this matter anyway. Pimps exploiting poor gullible females. Her own man was just as bad at times. How is this kind of stuff likely to shape young impressionable minds? People said that young people today had more resistance than is popularly believed. They'd need it. She didn't want to be thought of as a kill-joy, always going on about the same thing, but she had a duty.

"When are you serving Mass?" she said.

"Don't know," he repiled.

Wasn't that more of it? No matter how kindly you spoke to him. She'd keep her cool, as they say.

"Is it this evening or tomorrow morning you're serving?" she asked again.

"How should I know?"

Her anger seethed once more.

"Look, Ian, I'm asking you: will you be serving Mass at half-past seven this evening or not?"

"And I'm telling you I don't know. Isn't the list below?"

"That's the problem, it's not."

"Well where is it then?"

"That's what I want to find out!"

"Well how am I supposed to know? Maybe it fell off!"

"It didn't fall!" she fumed. "Go down and get it!"

"Get it! Get it! Do you think I've eaten it, maybe, and that I'm going to throw it up?"

"Just get it!" she said. "And go practise on the piano!"

He barked:

"I don't know where it is. Maybe it has legs!"

"Give over your cheek! It's a pity you're not half as

smart when you're wanted to be. In there with you and practise the piano."

"I hate the piano."

"You hate everything!"

Only at Grade Two. Six more grades to go; and then the diploma. If he got the diploma he could teach music. That would be something. Any qualification would be something the way the world was going, what with unemployment and all. But he wanted to give it up. He loathed his teacher. With a different teacher he could imagine continuing. But he told himself he wouldn't. His father said if they could get him a more understanding teacher who'd do modern songs with him. His mother disagreed. He'd have to continue at the School of Music. He'd never have got in there at all in the first place except she knew someone with influence. If he had to learn an instrument, he said, it would be the guitar. Too common, she said.

Anyway, she'd be keeping the situation under review. If she could persuade him to finish the year, then the holidays would be ahead of him and he might agree to start again. Year by year, she'd chip away at him. Her greatest fear was that he'd get his own way. That would have negative consequences, she believed. His father would be of little help. Once this negative decision was made it was made forever. What harm? That's what her husband said. Great harm, as she said herself.

She had to admit, however, that life doesn't always turn out as we wish it or as we plan it. She agreed, even if Ian was weak on the piano, he had other gifts. She believed he was clever, even if his cleverness was off the rails sometimes, his ideas about acting for instance, or his film 'Excalibur' if it comes to that. 'Excalibur – 2,000 years later'. He has written the script and chosen the actors. His own family would be the cast – his own family – along with neighbours and school mates. She herself would play the school mistress. Her husband would play Merlin. Merlin would have to climb a tall tree in the wood, wearing a flowing, black mantle and leap from tree-top to tree-top; and The Black Knight would have to take a flying leap from a castle battlement down into the river below. He explained that they wouldn't really have to perform these feats. He'd have stuntmen.

"How's it all going to come about?"

"What's the problem?"

"Who is going to be cameraman?"

"Himself or Daddy or whoever."

"And where's the camera going to come from?"

He had thought of that too. If they weren't going to buy one, and he'd pay back the loan later, they could hire one. He had worked it out that it would be cheaper to buy it at any rate. He'd buy it himself. He'd work for it: cleaning cars, mowing lawns, trimming hedges, buying groceries for old folks. He'd wash thousands of cars. He knew what else he'd do: he'd design wooden toys, he'd varnish and paint them and go around hawking them; if they gave him a loan of twenty quid.

"£20!"

"I'll pay it back!"

Did he think they were printing money? Let him earn it!

"Capital," he said.

"Capital. Earn the capital!"

"Capital like in a bank," he said.

He'd pay interest, he said. He would, she said.

He made a heap of this junk and tried selling it from door to door, trudging along with an old suitcase, packed with the stuff, price-tagged, and written on the case was a five month guarantee on every article sold. She advised him to lower his prices but he was incorrigible. They're too dear, no one will buy them, she said. If he sold them any cheaper, he said, there wouldn't be a penny profit. It would be a company with no assets.

"I'll say I'm selling them for charity," he said.

She warned him not to even think of it. She named neighbours whom he shouldn't approach, come hell or high water, and other neighbours not to be approached with a forty-foot pole. And not to bother neighbours with whom she was friendly either, making a tinker out of himself. What would he be but a huckster and a haggler and he knew well what reception she would give to any hawker that darkened her door. If he didn't heed her, she said, she wouldn't let him out the door at all.

What did he do but go straight to those neighbours that were on top of the black list; because they'd be the best buyers, which they turned out to be, he said. Under no circumstances whatsoever, she said. He'd have to give them back their money, she said. He'd have to apologise to them.

"Some of them bought two," he said.

God protect them!

"There was only one household that asked for their money back," he trumpeted, "because the yoke broke on them."

He told them he'd be happy to repair it. She reminded him of the five months guarantee.

"I'm prepared to repair an item but not to give money back," he said.

Why five months and not six, she thought to herself, but that wasn't the question she hurled at him out of the blue:

"What priest is on duty this week?

"I don't know," he said. "Father Daly, I think . . ."

Ian was thirteen. He had spent nearly a year now in secondary school. This was his third year as an altar boy. He wouldn't have had to serve a third year at all were it not for the new rules. He was happy with himself the day he was made an altar boy. "Apart from the priest I'll be the most important person in the church," he announced. The soutane added to his sense of self-importance. What pleased him most was the altar duty. Were it not for those little tasks the Mass would be a bore, he thought.

He was appointed head altar boy at the beginning of the second year. He had expected it. If he hadn't been chosen he would have thrown in the towel. As head altar boy he could allot duties: who would carry the thurible, who the paten, who ring the bell.

It was Fr. Daly who changed the rules and Ian's mother thought it was so as to allow the boy to benefit from the whole year. Fr. Daly hoped that Ian would have the makings of a priest. He became friendly with the family. Not overfamiliar, but he would visit them regularly and often bring Ian with him when doing the rounds of the sick in hospital. "I think it might do him good," he said, sagaciously. She said she'd bring it up with Ian.

She, too, hoped he would make a priest. She would like that. She wouldn't stand in his way. She didn't consider herself to be pious and wouldn't like to be thought of as such, but people spoke of her piety. She went to Mass, to confession and communion. She attended novenas and said the rosary. Did that mean she was pious? Thousands of others did the same. She believed in God, that was all – or, she believed she believed. It wasn't easy these days to be a priest; in a way she would be just as happy to leave it to some other young man. She contributed to other young men's noviciates and let God's will be done. Did Ian want to be a priest? Ian said he didn't know, but that he found the Mass somewhat tedious. But he liked Fr. Daly's car and was greatly impressed by the car-phone.

As it happened it was the Sunday for special prayers for vocations. She had put a pound in the basket going in. A visiting priest was present. He mounted the pulpit and greeted the congregation in a friendly manner. He was fat, paunchy, with cheeks the colour of claret.

"Parents must be very cautious in what they say to their children," he said. "Parents often deflect their children from a life in holy orders. To do so is a sin."

He might have been old but he spoke from the heart. He was honest.

"I ask parents, I petition them, not to stand between their own children and the life of holy orders, should any child of theirs desire such a life."

He changed the mood of his homily.

"It was much more difficult to become a priest in my time," he said. "It took seven years of hard study in those days and if you failed to get your B.A. after three years that was the end of it, you were shown the gate and not allowed back. I'm a priest now this forty one years and I can truly say I enjoyed every day of it. People say it's a lonely life, the life of a priest, but doesn't everyone feel lonely at some stage in their life? I would like to say to any young people who think they may have a vocation from God for the religious life, I would like to say to them to go to a priest and to talk to him because a priest won't be long giving them the advice they need. Young people, you are needed. The need has never been greater before."

As they made their way home, in no great hurry, Ian suddenly blurted out that he'd like to be a priest.

"When I'm big I'd like to be a priest," he said.

"As the fellow said, I will leave my wife and become a priest," said his father.

"What's the big joke?" said Ian.

"Why would you like to be a priest?" asked his mother.

"I don't know why, I just think I'd like to be," said Ian.

"You can talk to Fr. Daly as the priest suggested."

"Fr. Daly talks a lot about the priesthood, he thinks I'm

going to become a priest, he's always saying it."

"To whom?" said his mother.

"Everyone. He says it to the sick folk: here's a young man that's going to be a priest."

If he were a priest he wouldn't be married, thought his mother, no wife, no children. She hoped Fr. Daly wouldn't influence him overduly. Let him be happy, whatever he does, is all she asked.

"Every young person thinks he's going to be a priest," said his father, sensibly. "Thought so myself."

"Why don't you go to communion?" asked Ian. "Do you believe in God?""

"Give over that talk," said his mother.

"I was thinking if all else failed I could be a priest," he said.

"What failure are you talking about?" said she.

"I'd rather be an actor," he said, "though sometimes I'm afraid that God will call me and I start praying that he won't. Is that right?"

Ian didn't disclose to Fr. Daly that his interest in the priesthood depended on how he got on in other professions first, but Fr. Daly was interested in him more than ever before, proffering much advice. He now had regrets about the secondary school that Ian had begun attending. He had made known his choice to Ian's mother and there was plenty time to enroll him in the diocesan college but instead he was sent to the comprehensive school. It was closest. She herself would have preferred to send him to the Jesuits but they were on the other side of the city. The worst thing about the comprehensive wasn't that it was run by the laiety but that they had girls. That was the problem. But he would not be slack in his duties, ensuring that the boy receive constant clerical influence. He knew the chaplin in the comprehensive well and there was also a nun on the staff; he would ask them to keep a discreet eye on him.

Fr. Daly believed his schemes were working out wondrously well. What most gave him joy was Ian's steadiness of character. They'd go for a spin in the car and he'd give the boy prayers and pamphlets to read, all with excellent results: the boy was reading them, referring to them and asking for more. He gave him medals and scapulars to wear and it was plain to see how contented he grew with the passing of time. He was happy to see the boy's joy, his absolute contentment, his self-assurance. The boy had full confidence in himself and bore himself proudly. No harm in that, thought Fr. Daly.

Suddenly things took an horrendous course. Ian began to feel that the other boys were making fun of him. At first it was the older boys, then his own peers started on the same antics. They mocked and jeered. At first he didn't care, thinking it was simply a matter of envy, but then he began to hear the things they were saying.

They were saying Fr. Daly was bent. They wrote it down, on scraps of paper. Bent? In what way was he bent? What does it mean, 'bent'? He knew the word, but did it have another meaning? He checked in the dictionary and asked his father and mother what it meant. But he didn't mention that it was in the context of Fr. Daly that he wished to know the meaning of the word. Then he told his father. Suddenly it was plain to him. It was a great blow. Bent! He never imagined Fr. Daly to be anything like that. He was terribly confused. In one fell swoop he decided he'd never again be seen in Fr. Daly's company. But what the big boys were saying is that all priests were like that: each and every one of them, bent.

Overnight he lost his self-respect. He didn't want to serve Mass anymore. He wanted to ask his father did he know that every priest was as bent as a corkscrew.

"You were to call Fr. Daly."

He wanted to tell his mother there and then that he

never wanted to talk to that Papist ponce again. But he knew what she'd say to him: to watch his language and who was he calling a – what did he call him?

"I don't want to serve Mass anymore!" he said.

"What are you saying?" she said.

"I'm saying I'm done with serving Mass!" he said.

"Don't be talking nonsense!"

"I've done my three years and my sentence is up, full stop," he said, in control of himself.

"And what do you think Fr. Daly will say to all this?" she asked.

"I don't care," said Ian.

The Pheasant

The hurt still smarts. I twist and writhe with embarrasment. Perspiration pours from me in globules, running down my face. I wish to hide, to bury myself, to get out in the air on the road home on my bicycle. I see before me my raised hand; standing, crouched.

"Sit down, you booby!"

It was English class. We were doing 'The Wind in the Willows', Father Mitchell teaching us. A kind man, a good teacher. He was explaining the difficult words. As usual he'd put the word to the class. I never had my hand up, not until today. The word was 'peasant' and I knew it. Or thought I did.

"A bo-rd!" I said shyly.

The whole class roared with laughter.

"It's you, you eedjit!"

I had only seen one pheasant before that. We were spraying Lydon's potatoes when my father told me of the bird in the wood outside the wall. He was hiding in a clump of bushes. A strange bird! Such lovely colours! Like a bird in the school books, from some exotic parts, from Africa or South America.

My father said it was a cock pheasant. That there were birds like him in East Galway, reared to be shot. He was sorry he hadn't brought his gun with him.

"How do you know it's a cock?" I asked.

"From the comb!" he said.

"Oh!" I said.

The bird showed himself and disappeared, again and again. Little excursions out of the bush and back again. I thought a stone might do the trick. I placed my heather brush in the bucket of spray, put the bucket aside and found a nice stone. My father had the same idea but didn't act on it.

"If I got him right in the middle of his lovely red head, that should do the job nicely," I thought, hopefully.

My father had the spraying-machine on his back all the while, his old grey coat, hat and wellingtons.

"That red on his head isn't feathers at all!" he said.

"I know!" I replied.

"He must have come in from East Galway,"he said, "Jimmy must have taken him in."

We stood watching him for a long time. I was praying that I would land the stone on him.

"We should set a trap," I said.

My father said that a trap wouldn't do.

"Why not?" I asked.

"His leg would snap like a twig," he said.

I imagined a twig snapping in two.

"Wouldn't you go home for the gun?" I asked.

"He'd be gone!"

How strange he hung about so long, I thought. After a time I slowly, carefully, climbed over the wall. The beautiful bird flew away.

That was forty years ago. A year before I went east to secondary school. I thought I knew a lot about pheasants. After the boys had had their fun with me, after making me a laughing stock, I thought about it again. I thought maybe since Father Mitchell was from the town that he'd never laid eyes on a pheasant. That, in spite of all his learning, he hadn't said the word properly. That's why he said 'peasant' instead of 'pheasant'. That it was a printer's error in the book.

Poetry Reading

The spacious hotel function-room and the milling audience nearly took the wind out of Paul. As soon as he put his head in the door he knew he was going to wilt. Such a reaction was fairly typical, at times like this, but with his accustomed determination he knew he would succeed in correcting this little flaw of nature. Should he fail, it would only spur him on more passionately. Going home he always had renewed hope that his courage would never fail him again. Until the next challenge came his way, he would enjoy a carefree, spirited existence, nothing now could topple him – whatever it might be – because there he'd be with his photo in the paper, famous at last, having lectured somewhere about something or other, or delivered a stirring oration.

It was a rectangular function-room, the chairs arranged to the left of the door. Paul manouvered as far back to the rear as he could. He was always reluctant to sit too near the front; should he have something to say he would be in full view of the audience. However, with such a crowd gathered, he didn't rightly know where his navigation had brought him until he was seated for some time.

The table was positioned just inside the door, with a green cloth covering it. On it was a jug of water and two empty glasses lay by a microphone. Two chairs stood waiting.

'For the poet and chairman. Which one will drink the water? The poet I suppose!' thought Paul without delving any deeper into the mystery.

Though the poet's hour of glory had come, there was still no sign of him, or of the chairman. At least none of the assembled looked like a poet, or chairman. But why weren't there other poets here to listen to this illustrious bard? Maybe he wasn't that famous. How famous? He must be respected to have pulled a crowd like this. Some crowd! Every seat had a bum, almost, a few empty ones at the very front, one or two gaps here and there. Otherwise . . . some crowd!

They'd all have an opinion about the poetry and about the poet. At the moment they were chattering and muttering among themselves. They were all being very nice, very discreet, thought Paul. Bowing and scraping. Red-faced, some of them – the middle-aged ones looked ruddy – fortified by whisky, no doubt. Most of them conversing about poetry, determined to share what little they knew, especially to someone they didn't know.

Paul spoke to no one. He remained in his own cocoon and, as fragments of conversation entered his ear, wished for nothing more. Were he the poet how would he fare? Would he be able to respond to questions from the gentlefolk? Or would he be struck dumb? He'd like nothing more that to be able to stand at the table and address them boldly, vigorously. But no. Were he asked now to walk towards the table, what an Herculean effort it would be. He'd turn to jelly. His face flushed and he perspired at the very thought of it, fighting the concept with all his being. He crossed his legs and gave a little cough, or was it a groan? What did you need to know to be invited here; what did the poet know? How much more courage than he could muster at present was needed to accept such an invitation?

His musings were interrupted when five men entered the room. Among them one of his professors. He recognised three others as well, all from the University. He was embarrassed, looking at his own professor, even though he was some distance away. Would he be spotted?

Didn't he want to be seen, at first? Not that he had no other reason for being there! Would his professor think he was interested in poetry? Well, wasn't it obvious, by his very presence? Or maybe he'd say to himself: "Well who would believe it, O'Donnell from Tawnystraw; what's he doing here?"

The five of them conversed for a while, not without a sprinkling of humour, or so it seemed. Then three of them sat in the front row while the other two betook themselves to the table. One was a delicate man of meagre stature with a wanton beard. That was the poet. The chairman was a bull of a man with a neck to prove it. The poet procured a bottle from his coat and took a few swigs while the chairman introduced him to the audience. Between sentences he glanced at the poet, smilingly, as though not intending to offend the person he was referring to, as someone not sure of the veracity of his own speech. The poet was oblivious to all this, in a cosmos of his own. But as soon as the chairman sat down, the poet was on his feet.

Paul scrutinised him. Such a squirt to be a poet! You'd expect him to be rummaging in city dust-bins. Or in some attic, overwhelmed by spiders' webs, his face had such a withered pallor. At first his voice was faint, low, but soon became animated. Paul was keen to grasp his meaning, not knowing for sure if he did, or not, until everyone around him exploded in laughter. The poet was not joining in, as imperturbable as ever. He kept a straight face, as pale as when he started, though the chairman next to him was tittering noticeably. He spoke again and, once more, the audience collapsed. Paul had no notion why. How the devil a little scut like that could be so mockingly intelligent he simply couldn't figure out. He thought about it. Weren't most of the people he knew, who were anybody, insignificant in stature? Scraggy and bleary-eyed, you'd have to laugh at them, though if the truth be told it was they had the last laugh always.

The poet reclined in his chair under waves of laughter. He opened a volume of poems and was about to read when he remembered his medication and took a dram or two. He was in no hurry. He had intended to read a particular poem and then decided against it. He would read another instead, good, bad or indifferent; he couldn't say, as it was a long time since he had read it. But he had a vague idea it might be excellent. If not, no harm done: he'd read another. He muttered something when he came to the page with the waiting poem. He glanced at the front row and not knowing for sure if they thought what he had just said was funny or not – or whether they understood – he went on with the poem.

From time to time a word or a syllable would be drawn out. He gesticulated. Sometimes a pause would be impregnated with silence. Total silence signified the end of the poem. The audience was stumped for a second, or two. An eerie calm. Then applause broke out. The meaning of the poem had totally escaped Paul. Was he alone? Did anyone know what it meant? If questions were permitted, why was no one asking?

Then a woman stood up. She seemed to know her stuff, thought Paul. Maybe she was familiar with the poem? Or maybe what she was saying bore no relation at all to the text?

The poet produced some snuff. As he brought it to his nostrils, whispering commenced in the room. Was it about the poem? Paul looked at the poet. He had never seen such an unkempt beard. A home for abandoned lice, no doubt. The poet announced another title. He was about to read the poem when he thought of something. He began with an introduction, relating what prompted him to write the poem. The time and place. It was one of his favourites. Then he read it. All four lines! The fourth line he shouted.

A great wave of a shout, staring wide-eyed, excitedly at his audience. The chairman bolted upwards in his seat and shone an admiring gaze on the poet. He felt he should say something and did, but whatever it was the poet took no heed.

Others began to whisper and there was much head-wagging. Paul said nothing. He didn't know what was going on. He felt numbed by the thought that maybe he wasn't too bright, especially as he had read a book about poetry before coming.

"There's an awful lot I have to read yet," he said to himself. It always struck him that poetry was something very profound. If it wasn't hard to unravel it wasn't poetry. It had to be verse, merely. That much he understood at least. One day he, too, would have an intellect! He would write about matters weighty!

The poet was now in full spate but Paul didn't hear a word, rapt in his own thoughts. He remained oblivious to his surroundings until a blast of laughter shook him out of his reveries. What he saw was the poet's face, quite flushed by now but obviously content. A teenage girl asked a question about a poem. She spoke so clearly, elegantly that Paul imagined her to be uppity and clever. Though not as old as himself she appeared to be able to frame her question with ease. Bravely she stood there, indifferent to being the focus of attention. Paul felt nervous listening to her, she was so accomplished and self-possessed. He stole a glance at the professors. Were they watching her? He would have liked to have asked a question but wouldn't have had half of her skill. Hadn't he a question prepared in his pocket? That this girl was younger than him, that was the galling part. His heart began to pound.

Questions were now rolling from all sides . . . sensible questions . . . fearlessly, uninhibitedly. He was trying to remember the phrasing of his own question but it was a jumble. He began to feel fidgety. He took the piece of paper from his pocket and read the question. Too long, he thought. How could he stay on his feet that long? He shortened it by a few words. Still not happy with it. He was distracted by the chairman announcing a quarter of an hour's break – before the bar closed. He reminded them also that a volume of the poet's work was on sale at the door.

People rose slowly from their seats and thronged out of the function room. Soon there was no one left but Paul, and a girl who sat alone quite near to him. Paul felt stifled, almost crushed, while she appeared to be relaxed and breezy. She looked around her at the empty room, stealing a glance at Paul. He hoped she'd leave, disappear, as a flush came to his cheeks, staring blindly ahead like a school-boy chastised. No, he couldn't bring himself to say hello. All he could think of was when would she leave. It was she who spoke, unexpectedly.

"What do you think of him?" she asked.

"He's good," said Paul, unconsciously.

And he felt like an awful git, his voice must have sounded so tortured. He must say something else! But what?

"Will you come for a drink?"

She looked at him straight in the face and she seemed to glow, to brim.

"I will, thanks!" she replied.

On leaving she reminded Paul that the book was available for five pounds. Impulsively, not knowing why, he bought the volume.

"Let me show you a poem that I think is particularly good," she said, taking the book without ceremony.

"But, go buy the drinks first."

Paul went to the counter but had to stand in line, a somewhat raggedy line. Spruce barmen were busy popping corks and filling pints.

'This girl has the hots for me', thought Paul, surveying the mêlée. 'Who is she? She's nothing to write a poem about!'

His mind was racing, thinking what he'd say to her. When he returned with the drinks, he found he had nothing to say.

He seated himself beside her, brought the glass to his lips when she handed him the book.

"Tell me what you think of that!" she demanded.

Paul took the book, not being able to think what else he might do.

"I won't make head or tail of this," he thought. He looked at the poem but his mind wouldn't settle, relentlessly telling him 'I won't understand!'

'She'll know. I'm reddening in the face. What will I do?' churning through his head so that the lines were incomprehensible.

"So, what do you say?" she asked.

"Good, I'd say it's good!" said Paul as though confessing under duress. But fortune smiled on him: she didn't continue with the inquisition. She took the book of poems, as though it were her own, and began to explain to Paul why she thought this particular poem was so exceptionally fine. She was eloquent and Paul felt he was being tutored. But the breadth of her knowledge only crushed him more. What would he not give to be as knowledgeable. If he only could master the critical jargon. He had come across a lot of it in that primer on poetics. But it seemed she used the terminology differently – though he couldn't recall the exact usage. If only he could remember! And he recalled telling himself as he read the book that he would have to remember! The effort he spent trying to remember! He'd have to read the whole book again . . .

The girl continued talking. Paul's head was ringing

with poets and poems he knew nothing about. Eventually not a syllable of what she was saying reached him as by now she had delved so deeply that it was all turkey-gobble. He felt anxious when he realized that the break was almost over. It was as if the girl wasn't there at all as he grappled with the question in his pocket. Would he have the courage to stand up and ask his question? What kind of a nincompoop was he at all? He would love to be in bed at this moment. What misfortune brought him here? He might put the question yet. It wasn't a silly question, was it? But he wouldn't tell this girl that he intended to ask a question, it might only put him off.

People began to pour back into the room. Paul and the girl got up, but he decided to go to the toilet first. He had to look at his question again, in private. Once enclosed in the WC he took out the scrap of paper and began to read: "Mr. Chairman, I would like to ask . . ." If only he could say it here aloud and know how his voice sounded. "Mr. Chairman . . ." Anybody listening outside? No need for "Mr. Chairman . . ." Take too long, anyway it didn't sound right.

In case someone was waiting to use the loo he went out and made his way to the function-room. Just as he sat down the poet was about to recommence. He didn't feel quite as perturbed as before and the flushes had abated. As soon as people began questioning the poet, however, he became conscious of his own unasked question and his courage began to drip away from him. At least the girl who had joined him for a drink hadn't asked any question. Maybe only he alone knew how really good she was. Maybe others would think that he was her equal. Were they taking notice of the pair of them and saying:

"Those two haven't asked anything. They don't know how! They're only here to pretend they know what's going on!"

Hobnobbing – was that his game?

It was then that the excrement hit the instrument for exciting air. The girl beside him rose, composedly, to speak. It was a question that required a degree of volubility, which was easily at her command. She used words that Paul had never heard before. But he noticed that practically everyone was looking at her. Was her professor among them? She'd fly through her exams.

But the poet was brusque in his reply. Paul couldn't figure out why her question didn't elicit a more elaborate response. Was the question too difficult for him? Anyway, everybody had seen her. If they see her on the street wouldn't they remember this night? He would have to ask his own question. If it were over and done with and well executed, how happy he'd be!

More hands were up. He raised his own hand, tentatively. Immediately his heart went thump-a-thump. His lips became dry. He would stay seated while asking the question. That would give him courage. But then hardly anybody would see him. The questions being asked were far removed from his own. Was it a question at all? Was it relevant to the poet's talk? Maybe he shouldn't bother asking it? Wouldn't he be making an eedjit out of himself? Supposing they started laughing at him. In front of this girl, and his professor. What would happen to his exam? But then, his hand was just one in a forest. He hoped the chairman would see him. . . wouldn't see him. A question was taken from a man beside him. The man lifted himself up and stood erect. He thanked the poet, for starters. He thanked him for the knowledge he himself had received. Then he asked for more.

Lord above! Paul nearly had a seizure. It was his own question, he was listening to his own question!

The poet answered without delay. He spoke sensibly on the subject, adding a little dash of merriment to it. He said that it was a question with which he had wrestled over a period but could not honestly say he had managed to answer to his own satisfaction, if the question could be answered at all. Some day it will be, that was for sure.

Others added their voices to the same subject. The argument spread throughout the room – groups of two or more exchanging viewpoints among each other.

"That was my question," Paul said, shyly, to the girl, his heart skipping. His spirits dropped again. He had been plundered, cannibalised.

The poet read a few more poems. When he stopped he muttered something that raised a laugh. Soon the place was in joyous uproar again. Some had tears of laughter streaming down their cheeks. He made an attempt at a chuckle. A man craned towards him.

"What was that he said?" he asked.

Paul began to think.

"Don't know," he said, his cheeks suddenly hot.

The man accepted this explanation politely but Paul felt like a gobshite. Why in God's name did he laugh? Laughing and not knowing why. He must be a turnip-head of the first degree.

Soon afterwards the proceedings came to an end. Some people scooted off, others dawdled. Paul saw an authoritative-looking person walk towards the table. He extended a brown, sealed envelope to the poet and then to the chairman. Payment, no doubt, from the way it was received and Paul tried to figure out how much, or who got most. The poet more than likely.

Before leaving, many of those who had bought the volume went up for the poet's signature. As though under a spell, Paul joined the queue. Before him he saw people bowing and scraping and smiling – childishly, thought Paul. What difference would it make to have the poet's name on the book? That was girls' stuff. Naïvety. Sheer codology. Why was he standing there? Like a crowd of teenagers around a stage, hoping for a picture or a glimpse of their rock-idols.

Only two more ahead of him now. Suddenly he turned to leave. He lowered his head slightly, not looking at anyone – but he didn't care any more what they thought. He was happy to have found this courage. On the way home, hope began to return. Taking the question from his pocket he crumpled it and lodged it in a dust-bin. He had learned much in the course of the night. He was getting better! Even though he didn't ask his question it didn't matter. The day would dawn and he would ask a question, stand before a crowd, speak boldly, challengingly, and people would talk about him and he would fear no man alive.

Fragment

The old woman was sitting by the window, knitting, when the young man entered the kitchen. Without rising, she stretched out a hand. Her wrinkled face lit up.

"You're very welcome," she said.

The young man sat down. He raised his left leg and placed it on his right, the left shin resting on the right thigh. He held his left shin in his right hand and allowed his left elbow to settle on the table.

"I have the photos," he said.

"Oh now, aren't you great," said the old woman.

The knitting needles stood like the ears of an alert hare but her fingers securely held the dark garment where she had stopped. They looked at one another. Her face shone though her lips were pursed. For a while she forgot to avert her gaze. They smiled. The woman bowed her head, with fondness and reverence.

"Aren't you great!" she said again.

The young man shifted his position, somewhat abashed. Embarrassment flickered in his eyes.

"Where's himself?" he asked kindly.

"Out in the barn, working," said the old woman.

She nodded.

"He never gives up," said the young man.

He looked at her: bony, wizened; a scarf of rough cloth on her head like his mother wore long ago. A black shawl around her shoulders. Long skirt.

Through the window he saw the rain falling. Mist on the hills. Inscrutable trees. The whole countryside was a melancholy of mildew.

He got up, and went out.

The woman hung the kettle on the hook. Water gurgled under his shoes. The haggard was one sodden sponge of mire and dirt. Large drops of rain parachuted from the sycamore. They mottled his jacket. Withered leaves descended on the corn stack, sliding down the eaves. A cairn of rotted leaves took over a corner of the barn-roof.

"Oh, it's yourself," said the old man.

He was resting under a load of hay: the hay was like a gigantic armchair. Beside him was a fork. All he had on was his shirt and trousers. In spite of the weather his forehead perspired and the top half of his shirt was open.

The young man felt the peace of the barn. It was a dark world of its own. He heard the rain on the tin roof and the voice of the wind. A lulling voice. Sometimes a moan, and then a cry.

"There's a leak over there," said the old man, nodding in the direction of a corner from where he had taken out the hay, "and anyway I'm going to fill it up well down that end. You'd want to be careful or the wind would blow the roof off in the winter."

The young man looked out the door. The bare branches of the apple trees battling with the wind. A withered leaf flew down from the roof and landed just in front of him. A sad and beautiful world, he thought.

He turned to the old man.

"I have the photos," he said.

"You have, have you?" said the old man.

He gave a broad smile. He had only one tooth in his gummy mouth. He slid down from the hay in a trice.

He extracted the fork from it and put it standing against the wall.

"I'll leave it here now in case I forget again where I left it," he said.

Malheur

"Are you o.k.?"

"Do you think she's o.k.?"

"Is that girl o.k. I wonder?"

The girl didn't answer. Their eyes followed her down the street. She seemed to be lame. It was raining.

"She's drowned to the skin!"

"Not even wearing a coat!"

"Those young ones don't mind the rain, they're as daft as ducks; she probably likes being wet!"

"Would you say she's from up above in the college?"

"She could be on drugs or something."

"Pissed more than likely. Girls these days are just as bad as the boys."

"Worse! Drink more, smoke more."

"They certainly smoke more. There's few of the lads smoking."

"They feel they have to do it, to show they've a mind of their own, more is the pity."

"True for you!"

"Should I have offered her a lift?"

"She'd probably have told you to go and screw yourself."

*   *   *

The bell rang. Another day over. The pupils busy writing down what was left on the blackboard. The master loudly announced the homework. Books and pens hastily thrown into bags; bumping into each other, the pupils exchanged apologies.

Not every pupil was scurrying. Teresa was in no hurry. Slowly she copied from the blackboard, slowly noted the homework. A large clumsy scrawl. She was sensitive to her own slowness, painfully aware of the others still in the classroom. Among them was Oonagh. Using her, pretending to be her friend, that was Oonagh. She mustn't have had any other friend this evening.

"Are you ready?"

"Almost."

Teresa began to hurry. She was pleased that it was for her that Oonagh was waiting, if only to ask a favour. She was angry that she allowed Oonagh to annoy her. The leech! Her mother has told her not to be crass with people, that it was no wonder she had so few friends. She had told her mother in no uncertain manner that she had enough friends. But her mother was right. She often ran off to her room in tears.

Her eyes smarted. They were tired, somewhat sunken in her head, after the day's tribulations; the insults she had to endure, the shame and embarrassment she was caused to feel. It had been a bad day. She wanted to be finished with school, with the school she was attending at any rate.

No other school could be as bad. St. Belinda's was nice, it had nice teachers, the girls were agreeable, not always picking on one another. She would have good friends there. Oonagh wasn't a friend, she was nothing more than a bimbo who thought too much of herself. She wanted to go to Belinda's from the first but she wasn't allowed. Her mother had other ideas.

Who wrote that on her seat: 'Teresa O'Shea is 100% in love with David O'Malley?' It was so embarrassing.

"Hurry, girls!"

"How's it going, Teresa?"

"Fine!"

She tried to smile. Her greeting had revived her spirts a

little. She didn't know if she wished to spurn or welcome Onagh. Well, her company was better than none. Oonagh held the door open for her. She felt a sudden affection for her. Maybe she wasn't quite as bad as she had thought.

Some of her fellow-pupils were getting into their parents' cars, fine flashy cars purring sweetly. Others walking off in groups, gossiping. She didn't like them; all they did was chat about boys and tease her, about David O'Malley. They depressed her. Pained her. She couldn't even look at him, though he appeared to be everywhere. She hated him.

She lived near the school. Oonagh lived a little further away. Oonagh was so lazy she'd often take the bus. Sometimes, when Oonagh walked, she wouldn't bother calling for her, to walk with her. Oonagh was using her.

"Never say that about anybody!"

"Why shouldn't I ?"

"Do you hear me?"

"I'll say what I like!"

"Nobody will be friends with you!"

"They will!"

"They won't!"

"Would you shut your fat gob!"

"You'll regret it!"

"I won't, o.k.?"

"You will – when it's too late!"

Teresa slunk to the bedroom, tears on her cheeks.

Oonagh could be tolerable sometimes. She could be nice when she wanted to. There were times when you could talk to her. She was pleasant when she wanted something. She had lent Oonagh her dungarees. They didn't suit her. She was too big, too plump. Oonagh never lent her anything.

"Do you like Mr. McSweeney?"

"He's not the worst."

"I like the way he asks you 'how are you gettin' on?"
"Yeah . . ."
"Did he ever ask you that?"
"I wouldn't want him to."
"I like the head on him. Nice head."
"He's an ould fella."
"I wonder what age he is?"
They stopped at the school gate to allow a car to go by. The road turned sharply outside the gate. It was dangerous the way cars whizzed by. There had been many complaints about the absence of a lollipop-lady.
"Seen David today?"
Teresa startled and pouted.
"Don't want to see him!"
"Would you like to marry him?"
"Would not!"
"What age would you like to be when you get married?"
"I mightn't marry at all!"
"What would you like to do later on?"
"I haven't the foggiest."
"I'd like to be a doctor. Or an oceanologist!"
"What's that?"
"An oceanologist?"
"Oh . . . yes . . ."
"You have to . . ."
"I'm sure it's easy . . ."
"Oh, it wouldn't be easy . . ."
"I'm sure it would . . ."
"Not going to get it anyway, too many points required."
"Well I certainly wouldn't get it."
"I'll fail."
"I'll fail every subject."
"I'd like to be a model."
"Oh yeah, me too."

"T'would be fab."

"Brillo."

"Rich . . ."

"Wow! Be alright wouldn't it?"

They laughed.

"Flash clothes, big car, a mansion. What kind of car would you like? Where would you like to live? I'd like to live in the country."

"I wouldn't, too dirty."

"There's places that aren't dirty. Wouldn't like to marry a farmer. Would you?"

They screeched with laughter.

"My ma thinks I'll be a teacher."

"Wouldn't like that."

"But I'll fail. I know I'll fail."

"Me too."

"I'll fail every subject."

"Me too. Well, maybe not every subject . . ."

"What won't I fail in d'ye think?"

"Haven't a clue, I think I might fail them all."

"Me too."

"I wonder what it would feel like, to fail every subject?"

"You wouldn't get a job."

"You wouldn't have a tosser."

"A few bob on the dole."

"Hate that. How much? Roughly?"

"I'd like to be an architect, or a vet. Wouldn't like to be a dentist. Nobody would want to visit you. Imagine spending every day looking into somebody's mouth."

"Do you like Mr McSweeney?"

"What are you saying?"

"I like the way he speaks."

"He might give you a pass."

"I always pass that subject."

"I'm going to buy new Docs on Saturday."

"I might too."

*   *   *

"Don't say you're eating again?"

"I'm not fat!"

"I never said you were."

"But you hinted at it."

"All I said was you're eating too much. You've eaten a pizza already today!"

"Pizz-off!"

"You had a croissant too!" her mother said.

Though Teresa lacked confidence among her peers she could speak her mind to her mother. She liked correcting her mother.

"Croissant is French. You don't pronounce the 't!"

The funniest of the lot was 'gateaux'. Her mother pronounced the 'x' Her mother was a social embarrassment.

"You're always implying I'm fat. Others tell me I'm willowy."

"Oh, what do they care how you look? For all they're concerned you could look like the back of a mountain."

"Oh, shut your face!"

"Go up and do your study!"

"I've friends – which is more than can be said of you!" retorted Teresa.

Suddenly she felt terribly mixed up. Miserable. She closed the bedroom and cried her eyes out.

After a while her sobbing subsided. She sat up in bed. She had no friends, she thought to herself. She cried again, then went downstairs. Her mother was still in the kitchen, washing the dishes in the sink.

"You're the one who doesn't care!" said Teresa.

"Get up the stairs and do your study and don't be making a fool of yourself!"

"Who's the fool? I hate you!"

She slammed the door behind her.

"Close the door properly!" her mother shouted after her. "Do you not know yet how to close a door? Not one of ye can close a door properly!"

"Close it yourself if you're such an expert!" Teresa yelled back.

She despised her mother. She couldn't stand her brother either. She'd love to see them all dead.

"Teresa! Teresa, come down here!" her mother shouted.

Teresa paid no heed to her.

"Teresa, do you hear me saying to come down? Do you hear me calling you? Teresa, your mother is calling you!"

Her mother heard her muttering something.

"Say that again and you'll hear something from me!"

"Oh, will I now, mother?"

"There's not one of ye . . . Teresa! Teresa, I said!"

"Ah shut your face!"

"I'm tellin' ye . . ."

She darted from the hall to the kitchen, to get the wooden spoon. It was a long time since she had used it. She often thought of it. What else could she use? Be the hokey, she'd use it now and use it to effect.

"Open that door!"

She got no answer. She gave the same order again. Still no answer.

"Maybe it's deaf you are?"

"Maybe I'm not."

It was the indifferent, matter-of-fact tone of the reply that incensed her mother even more. Brat! The arrogant brat!

"After all I've done for you, after all I've given you!"

"Nothing, that's what I've been given."

Again, the same unperturbed tone of voice.

"Open that door!" said her mother, wearily.

"This isn't the end of it I can tell you," she said and went back down to the kitchen.

Standing alone in the kitchen she gathered her thoughts and then decided to plug in the kettle and make a cup of tea. Were all daughters like hers? Were other mothers able to communicate, to have a conversation? Why was Teresa so intransigent? Whatever one did for her she couldn't be satisfied. 'I never get anything! Who cares about me?' After getting everything: a new blouse on Saturday, new Docs, new dungarees. She poured herself a cup of tea and opened a box of biscuits. Not a biscuit left! She felt angry again, in the pit of her stomach. The box of biscuits she had hidden, hijacked again. Not a crumb left! The Micados, the Kimberleys, the Coconuts, the Fig Rolls – robbed!

"Teresa! Teresa? Where are all the biscuits gone?"

The same tactics: no reply.

"Teresa! Do you hear me up there? Teresa!"

"I can't hear you, mother, I'm deaf!"

She tried to overlook that remark and speak in a reasoning tone.

"Where could the biscuits have gone?"

"Ask your darling son!" came the reply from above as her daughter slammed the bedroom door.

What a daughter to have, what kind of person is she at all, said the mother to herself. People told her she'd grow out of it, that it was only a phase, that girls were much worse than boys in that way. Well, she was worse, no doubt about it. Sometimes she'd think of bringing her to a doctor, that maybe she needed help. 'She'll grow out of it . . .' Well it was time she did, bordering on seventeen.

When she opened the fridge she discovered there wasn't a yoghurt left. All eaten! By Teresa. Was it any wonder she'd gotten heavy? Something had to done.

'Oh yes, blame me!' She could hear her daughter's voice. Maybe she wasn't the culprit after all, maybe it was

Damien; maybe she blamed Teresa unfairly? If only it were so. She would go to her with open arms, hug her and ask forgiveness. All her problems would be over. Mother and daughter would hit the town together, if only her daughter were different somehow, or the same as everyone else, if only she weren't overweight, they could go to a restaurant, hotel or café, order what they like and enjoy the day and each other's company. To be like any other mother and daughter: to have a civilized conversation instead of behaving like weasels. To ask her about her friends, the type of music she liked, the disco scene.

Teresa didn't go to discos. She went once and that was more than enough. They never talked about it. She asked about it and knew from the reply that it wasn't worth teasing it out. She hardly remarked on it at the time. She was quite happy that Teresa didn't ask permission to go again. She can wait, she said to herself, until she'd done the Leaving Cert. After that she could enjoy herself. Lately she had begun to worry. When she heard people talking about discos she thought it would be nice if Teresa asked to go, showed some interest. Not that she was killing herself studying. The opposite.

"Does Oonagh go to discos?"

"Don't talk to me about that one!" she warned.

"Like to go to the disco tonight?"

"Don't pretend you're interested in me."

She tried to restrain herself. It wasn't easy.

"I love your manners!"

"Nobody gives a tinker's curse about me."

And then the flood of tears, running out from the kitchen.

Her mother heard the argument going on upstairs. She heard Teresa's rasping voice. That same high-pitched tone. Waste of time asking her to lower her voice, she'd only shout the more.

'Ye're always picking on me,' she'd say.

She'd gone into Damien's room, looking for help with something; instead she began insulting him. He was telling her, yelling at her, ordering her to get the hell out of his room. She didn't. She stood there, bombarding him with abuse. Could you blame him for not helping her? Even if he did help her, the only thanks he'd get would be insult.

"God look down on us . . ."

She looked at the television but her mind was elsewhere, hoping the commotion upstairs would subside, that Teresa would leave and go to her own room. No such luck.

It continued, the accusations, one bettering the other, yelling. Where would it all end? Would she grow out of it as they said she would? At what age? No sign of it yet. If she'd only be reasonable she could be given some help.

The cursed Leaving Cert! If only she could get into teaching. Maybe it was an old-fashioned idea – to hell with fashion – it was a fine vocation for a girl: short working hours, long holidays, decent pay.

She listened more carefully. Teresa was still in Damien's room. Though he was a kind-hearted boy, she was afraid he'd use too much force to throw Teresa out of the room.

"You're full of shite!"

Her mother felt a gag of revulsion at such shameful talk. Disgraceful coming from anybody. Her own daughter . . . where did she pick up such language?

How often had she asked Teresa to restrain her tongue.

"Shove your head up your arse!"

The mother flew upstairs. She wouldn't put up with such filthy talk.

"What kind of language am I hearing?"

"What did I say, mother?"

"Get out of that room!"

"I will if I want to."

"Go to your own room!"

She caught her daughter by the shoulder and tugged. She was as heavy as a granite boulder.

"Take your hand off me, mother!"

She loathed being called 'mother'.

"Oh, I can't call you 'mother' now? I thought you *were* my mother. I'd prefer if you weren't. I wish I were adopted so I could go and look for my real mother. You're the worst mother on earth! I'd like to go to the phone and ring up –"

"Do!"

"I will one day!"

"You're a wonderful daughter!"

"I'd like to get the hell out of here!"

"Off you go! Go on! You won't be gone long!"

"I'll piss off out of here one day. I'll be gone before you know where I am!"

"Suits me fine."

"That's it then."

Teresa was crying, sitting at her desk in the bedroom. She wished she were dead. Her mother's tirade ploughed through her head: 'if you just worked,' 'if you even made an effort!' She did work, she did make an effort, she worked hard. 'All the money spent on you! Putting you to college so that you'll be somebody one day!' She heard the music from the radio in the kitchen, faintly. And Damien's Hi-Fi, barely audible, from his room. But if she turned on her Hi-Fi what would be said? No wonder she couldn't do a stroke of work. 'How can you study if the radio's blaring beside you?' That was never said to Damien. It wasn't a just world. Why was she given lesser intelligence?

The walls of her room were covered with posters: Johnny Depp, Christian Slater, Jason Priestly.

Johnny Depp was thrown out of school because of alcohol and drugs, aged twelve. At thirteen he slept with a girl. He left home at sixteen. He married when he was twenty. She'd like to able to leave home and family and launch out into the wide world. It would be easy to do that in America, she thought. Tom Cruise. She had a photo of Tom Cruise. She thought he was beautiful, a lovely face, adorable eyes. In the photo he was kissing a child's toe: the child was lying on its back wearing only a nappie. She'd like to have a child of her own.

Loads of teddies and soft-toy kittens sat on her bed and on the shelves. A pile of letters and cards received from friends and relations over the years. Her school-tie on the floor. A poster of a young girl, her arms hugging a big shaggy dog, hung over her desk with the bold legend:

IF YOU LOVE SOMEONE SHOW IT.

Another poster showed the dog only. The dog was crying:

NOBODY LOVES ME!

Eventually she decided to go to Damien again, though she hated doing it, A belly-ache, literally. Every time she hoped it would be the last, that she'd manage to do all her lessons without asking his help. She did try and it was unjust to suggest otherwise. That's what she liked about Mr. McSweeney. He knew she was a tryer and encouraged her: 'We can only do our best! To do one's best Teresa, that in itself is more than enough.'

"It's only fifteen days to my birthday," she told Damien, as matter-of-factly as she could say the words. She didn't want another argument.

"Oh, wow!" he said.

Her heart sank.

"Will you tell your friends?" she asked.

"Why would I do that?" he grinned, curiously.

"Just . . ."

"Just what exactly?"

"I hate you!" she blurted, turned round and slammed the door on the way out.

She closed her own door firmly and started to cry. She cried for a long time and then went down to the kitchen.

"Don't start eating again," said her mother.

"Who said anything about eating?"

She began to give out about Damien, that he wouldn't help her with her lessons.

"She never asked me!" protested Damien.

"You're lying through your teeth!" she said.

"You didn't ask me!" Damien said firmly.

"Liar! Liar!"

"She asked me to tell my friends about her birthday!"

"Liar! Liar! why should I say such a thing?"

"Why indeed!"

"You could have asked him nicely," interrupted their mother.

"I never asked him!" screamed Teresa.

"About your lessons," her mother said.

"She didn't ask me to help her with her lessons," said Damien.

"She doesn't know how to behave in a civilized manner," said the mother.

Teresa kicked Damien in the shin.

"Now she's kicking me!"

She kicked him again. Damien pushed her aside.

"Stop that Damien!" screamed Teresa.

"Go fuck," said Damien.

"You pig-shit!" she roared at him.

"You're the shit," said Damien, "and you stink!"

"God look down on us!" said the mother. "What in God's name –? If I hear . . . what in the . . ."

"I'd be alright if I hadn't you as a mother! It's not my fault! You brought me into this world!"

"That a body should put up with this!"

"I've had to put up with ye for sixteen years," screamed

Teresa, her eyes blinded with tears as she stormed out of the kitchen.

"You're not allowed watch television," said her mother. "Go straight up to your room!"

"Who said anything about television?" she shouted back. "Jesus H. Christ!"

Her mother heaved a sigh.

"Where did we get her?"

"I heard that!" said Teresa, opening the door again. "From your belly that's where! Out through your smelly arse!"

*   *   *

It was a sultry day. Teresa was in her room, doing some study. But her mind was not on her books. Though her head was bowed she appeared to be gazing at some distant object. Her eyes were transfixed in a glassy stare, as though contemplating an inscrutable mystery. Nor was she listening to the faint drone of the Hi-Fi. Oonagh had told her she looked to all the world like a farmer's wife. She had been pestering her about David O'Malley. Her mother had said she was obese. As fat as a fool. She had said she had no friends and was it any wonder. She had said she was turning into a haystack. That she was ill-mannered, as bold as brass, an ill-tempered hussy. Was she really so horrendous? Yes, she was. She felt guilty about 'the rake of money spent on her.'

A knock on the door. She was about to say 'go away,' but it was her mother and she was already in the room.

"Like to come for a spin?"

"No."

"Such a lovely day."

"Must study."

"You need a break, we won't be long."

"I'm not going."

She belched.

"Oh stop it!" said her mother.

Teresa burst into tears.

"It's only a habit," said her mother.

"No it's not . . ." her voice was thin, barely audible.

"You won't come then?"

"Got to study."

"Study a bit . . . then call Oonagh, ask her to come over."

"Don't want her."

I'm not even talking to her, the bitch, she said in her own mind.

"You won't come so?"

"I don't want to."

"Will you be alright on your own?"

"Who cares?"

"We do! We're for your good if you could only get that into your skull."

Her mother hesitated, went to the window, looked out. Teresa hoped she would leave.

She heard the front door close and the car-engine purring. She rushed to the window to see if Damien was in the passenger-seat, to make sure she was alone in the house.

She was agitated but knew exactly what had to be done. She would leave the note on her mother's bed.

She closed the house-door behind her, checking it was locked. All thoughts were now banished from her mind except for the location and the act itself. She could picture the location clearly. She walked by the river. She would remain inconspicuous on the path, the path that led to the open fields, the seldom-walked fields. The river meandered ahead and soon the current would grow stronger and the river wide and deep. Big boats navigated up the estuary as far as here.

She hesitated. The sun unexpectedly vanished behind dark clouds and a pall descended on the surrounding countryside. The water looked cold. A drum-peal of thunder. It began to rain. Raindrops on her cheeks mingled with tears.

The Shepherd

He was called Páidín an Mhaoir as a young fellow and the name stuck. Born in Tamhnach Ard, he spent his life there. He never lived anywhere else. He was born in the same house, an ordinary thatched cottage, where his father and grandfather before him came into this world. Páidín was the youngest of four brothers. The other brothers all emigrated, except for Mártan who married below in the glen. Now they were all dead, though Mártan's family and wife lived on in the glen.

We went to visit Páidín, out on the Clifden road. Having gone some miles, we turned right, down an old boreen with a babbling river on the left: now flooded, it raced noisily on its way. It wasn't too deep but it was full of rocks, churning the waters to foam as it hastened ever onwards.

The boreen was steep but you knew it would come to an end. How winding it was! This was a craggy area, bushes looming here and there, an entangled world. What really surprised us was the amount of fine new houses, spacious bungalows, all built on the side of the boreen; it must have been quite a job levelling the sites. Old rock-encrusted land, how could it invite such fancy houses?

The ground grew steeper, bushes fewer. Now only the occasional house was visible. After a while no house at all, just unending moor. This is what we expected, this is what we were told, that Páidín an Mhaoir's place was out on its own.

We left the car by a bulge in the boreen; the way had become pot-holed, and we continued on foot. Soon we came to the grassy upland that gave Tamhnach Ard its name; there it was, ahead of us, on a hill crowned with conifers. The house was in the middle with tiny fields sloping down on each side, a checkboard of tiny plots divided by stone walls. In one of them was a suckling calf and a few young heifers with little to eat; an old donkey stood alone in another little field facing the level ground around the house, the picture of misery, sad, hungry, his lower lip fallen. Our presence only registered with him for an instant. A flock of geese ruled over another field which had a pond.

The roof of the house was in a bad way, partly only mud, and birds paraded on it in search of worms. Páidín would soon feel the drip, if it wasn't leaking already. We noticed the wrens toing and froing in front of the house, in and out of holes in the stone wall as though they were mice; they'd hop down on the walls of the house and take off again like a surprised leprechaun.

Where could Páidín be? Out on the moor, we supposed. He didn't appear to be anywhere in the vicinity of the house; not a dog barked – and Páidín had two. Would our trip be in vain? He wasn't expecting us. But we'd stick around and see.

We went east, a back-way between two walls, a short way. At the end was a bright moor extending east to the river. Beyond that the russet moor opened, stretching as far east as east goes, to the eastern horizon and beyond. There were a good few sheep scattered here and there.

It wasn't long until we heard a whistle. Long and rolling like that of the curlew. This we took to be Páidín, whistling to his dogs, giving them instructions. Shepherds had a whistle all of their own, it was said. Páidín had it, they said, a language of signals and messages, a language uttered if they were trapped or needed help; a whistle that could carry for miles, it was said, if you knew the signals.

Who else could that speck in the far distance be but

Páidín? He approached us with a sure gait. The two dogs accompanied him, running a few yards ahead and returning, startling the odd sheep.

We strolled down, as casually as we could, where a small bridge spanned the river. A dog stood on the far side, lifted its head, and howled. It howled a few times in succession. Páidín had an old raincoat on. He was of medium height wearing wellingtons and a battered caubeen. His face was mustardy, wrinkled and stubbly.

"God be with you!" we said aloud, not knowing if we should call him by his first name.

"God be with ye and Mary!" he replied calmly. He wasn't displeased to see us.

"Fine weather!"

" 'Tis fine!" he said.

"You'd be Páidín Ó Conaola – Páidín an Mhaoir?" we asked as we approached.

We shook hands. A calloused hand. Huge hand like a shovel.

"We read about you," we said and we smiled.

"You did? About this clown?" he said mockingly.

"Oh you're no clown!"

"A clown about town!"

"You're famous!"

"The Lord between us and all harm!"

We walked back towards the house. The ground seemed slippier than the last time. The wind felt sharper than before. Back again in front of the house we couldn't help noticing the wrens, flying in all directions like fairies playing hide-and-go-seek.

"There seems to be a fair rattling of wrens about," we said. They were most entertaining, their giddy flight, alighting on this or that, and away with them again. As frisky as little children.

"They have nests in the eaves," Páidín informed us.

"Oh!"

"Them eaves are infested with wrens!" he said. "I'd meant to do more thatching but it'll have to wait now until spring. Lately I've a fear of the ladder. Young fellows came up here from the glen on Wren Day, looking for birds; there's not many houses like this left. All you have to do is put your hand into the nest at night and put them into a jar, or a box, and put a lid on it. They do the rounds of the houses then the following day, chanting:

'The wren, the wren, the King of all birds,' and collect a few pence . . . "

"Poor wrens!" we said, half-jokingly, but Páidín would have none of it.

"Very few of the wrens die," he insisted. "One or two maybe, that's all, if they exhausted themselves hopping about, but they're let go again. They'll stay quiet if a dark lid is put on the jar. I don't like seeing them die at all."

As we went to lift the latch on the door, he cautioned us:

"Don't mind the state the house is in, I've a few sheep inside. Someone like myself has to be sheep-doctor and shepherd rolled into one."

Hooves knocking on the floor is what first we heard. Two small skittish sheep. They hadn't the whole kitchen to themselves, penned by wooden boards in one half and the door to the east wide open .

"I've more in the room," he said.

Mountain sheep with little stumps of horns, the two of them scurried off into the room. The kitchen was strewn with branches of red holly.

Páidín took the covering from the embers.

"It's nearly gone out," he said, "but I've been away since morning."

He poked the embers with the tongs, raking it forward. There was life in it yet. He put on a few sods and hung the kettle over them.

"We'll have a drop of punch when she boils," he said softly, as though talking to himself.

"Indeed," he said, "when you live alone like I do you have to be vet and sergeant as well."

True, anyone with two hundred sheep on the moor with no sheep-folds and precious little grass-land. The moor was sodden in winter. His task would have been impossible but for those who came to help him, to brand, to dip, to bring to fair. Mártan's sons came to help him. He'd mostly sell them at home of late and a good price he got too. Better than cattle. Cattle wouldn't thrive on his land anyway. He had no complaints, a thousand thanks to God. It was plain sailing. There was a time he'd do his herding on horseback, like his father before him, but that was no longer the case. It wasn't worth keeping a pony.

Páidín took three mugs and an opened bottle from the dresser, poured three measures and added water from the kettle and some sugar.

"The poteen is a rogue," he said, "but ye needn't fear this, I've been drinking it all my days."

"*Sláinte!*" We toasted our host.

"*Sláinte mhaith anois agus fad saoil!*" said Páidín, wishing us good health and a long life. "A wee drop of the best!"

"More power to your elbow!" he jested.

"And to all other parts!" he laughed.

The sheep gathered at the door and their heads turned our way, inquistively. Páidín spoke kindly to them.

"They're all the company I've got," he said.

"You don't go out much?" we asked. "If you don't mind our asking?"

"Don't mind a bit."

"You wouldn't go out visiting or anything?"

He said he might go down to Mártan's or east to Johnny Eoghain's for a bit of a chat and maybe even a drop of the hard stuff. Johnny himself was dead by now but his eldest

son did a round now and again. He might have the odd
visitor at night and they'd talk about the old ways. No
place on earth could entice him more than the old stone
wall at night, his overcoat on, under the shelter of the trees.
He'd often sit alone there.

"Sometimes I'd spend a long while there before going
in, looking at the lights of the big town and all the lights of
the world," he said. He'd pick out quite a few places that
would not be visible by day.

"Lights are great company when your're on your own
and they're nicest of all on a moonless night. Though I like
the moon as well, the white nag in the lakes . . ."

How would he spend Christmas? Would he prepare his
own dinner or have someone do it for him? Would he go to
Mártan's widow or would they send a meal up to him? He
preferred to make his own meals and wasn't lonely. He was
well used to being alone.

We heard commotion from geese. His own geese? Yes
and no. The wild geese were conversing and Páidín's geese
calling back. The wild geese were flying low on account of
the gale. They might settle in the quagmire. Did he go
fowling? He had enough geese of his own. He used to fowl
with his father. His father would go out at night and Páidín
with him; they'd travel east and stay secluded for the night
in a shelter.

"On a starlit night you'd spot a goose or two and hear
their cackle approach. Sometimes they'd settle, othertimes
not, or settle too far away from you and you'd be dithering
with nothing to do."

He was very young then. His father killed foxes and so
did he. There was no lack of foxes about and they
slaughtered hens galore. You couldn't keep hens any
longer. They'd kill ducks as well or lambs that weren't
sturdy. They'd prowl on sheep at lambing time.

"Foxes come around to the house at night and fight with

the dogs. On cold, quiet nights you'd hear them bark, a sharp lonely cry like the wail of a banshee."

Worst of all were the vixens.

And it wasn't only foxes that came. Badgers, too, would come out of their dens. The dogs would never attack them but they'd bark at them and scamper off.

"It's a quiet place," he said. "Thieving minks come from the river when frost is on the ground and they'd come up to the threshold! The mink has no fear of man," he said. "They'd look you in the eye. Oddly enough I like them, I'm very happy in their company."

Nothing could be worse than snow, he said, though he admitted he liked it as long as it didn't last too long. But it was very dangerous and most years there'd be a big fall. Snow was bad for sheep giving birth and many a snowy night he spent out in the hovel. He'd often be stuck there. We asked him did the hovel have any furniture and he burst out laughing.

"Yerra what," he said, "unless you'd call the stump of a candle furniture."

Wouldn't he want to sit down?

"You'd sit on a stone," he said.

"You wouldn't be lonesome?"

"Not a bit."

"Or afraid?"

He burst out laughing again.

"Of what?"

"And what would you be thinking about?"

"You'd be thinking about the snow, or the fog," he said, "looking out to see would it be rising, was it getting bright."

Even if he had to spend the whole night there – and many is the time he did, it didn't matter to him, hadn't he the dogs as company. Maybe the stone would get uncomfortable and he'd stand, go out, come in again, sit down again and pass the night like that or he might even doze off. There might be a bag of bedding there and he'd lean his head on it, or a drop of the hard stuff and he'd have a few swigs, just enough to keep the heat in him.

What pastimes did he have as a youngster?

"Herding sheep!"

"When you were a lad?"

"Herding sheep!"

He might go house-visiting some nights.

What was his dearest memory? Any special memory? He stirred.

"Isn't it odd," he said, "but there's one thing that stands out in my memory and that was a clutch of green eggs that I came upon, unexpectedly, out on the moor; as green as the grass beyond, or as cabbage; five of them, each beside the other in a small round nest on the ground, the eggs of a whinchat! Do ye know the bird I mean? Well, I didn't know myself until I talked to this man who came to me and it was he that told me, the eggs of a whinchat. He was a birdman from the university and he told me a lot and do you know I was fierce interested. Well, I always thought, and still do to this day, that they were the prettiest things I ever saw and isn't that something now for a countryman to say who's spent all his life on the moor, and had to be informed by a city man!"

"That's life for you," he said. "And, as they say, life is a quare hawk. I'm getting old now but even so I've no fear of old age or death. I had my spin. I'm as happy as Larry."

Would Mártan's sons take over, did he think? He thought they'd sell the place to the forestry.

When we left Páidín an Mhaoir that evening the light was draining from the sky and house-lights twinkled in the distance, the town-lights coming on. Since he had to close the goose-cote and milk the cow, he didn't come down as far as the car with us. He said his good-byes on the rise. We said we hoped we'd meet again. We didn't. A few years later we heard what happened: he was found, frozen cold, on the icy moor, an opened bottle of poteen in his coat pocket.

Ambition

He took off his clothes, folding each item carefully and placing them in the basket; he had brought a plastic bag for his shoes. He never liked putting them with his clothes, however clean the soles. Shoes always had a pong, he believed, whether you powdered them or not and, yes, he did use powder.

"Hardly need to put them in the basket," his companion, Dick, said.

"Put them in the basket," said Tony.

Was it advice or an order?

"Hardly need to bring the basket with us," said Dick.

"Bring it with you," said Tony.

"Who'd rob it?" said Dick.

"You'd never know," said Tony. "I know this place better than you do. They'd pluck the eye out of a duck. Things have a way of disappearing. I'd be more worried if there wasn't a sign of a thief about."

Tony was a big bronzed fellow, hairy-chested, paunchy, built like a tank.

"I don't get it," said Tony. "How ignorant so-called educated people can be, how innocent. Me? I know people too well. Give a bit, take a bit, that's the way it is with them. But I want nothing of it."

Tony was heavy-footed, Dick sprightly. Tony called Dick a fat slob, though he wasn't like that at all.

"I'll look after my own and would advise you to do the same," said Tony.

They stopped in their tracks at the pool door, Tony standing in Dick's way.

"Holy God," cried Tony, "sufferin' Jesus!"

A small group taking swimming lessons, three women and a man.

"Mother of perpetual suckers, would you look at 'em," he moaned.

"Ever see the likes? Three hens and a cock!"

"Look at 'em! Three nuns, I'd swear – and a monk."

"Scared shitless by the looks of them!"

"A day out from the convent. God save us all."

He blessed himself.

"Come on," says Dick.

"Up this way; we'll keep away from them," said Tony.

Up they went towards the deep end. Dick dived in. Tony dipped his left leg cautiously in the water and out again in a trice, mimicking a young girl.

"Aw Mammy, I can't – I'm afraid!"

Then he walked straight into the water and sank like a stone. He popped up again in the same place.

"I stood on the bottom," he said.

"Keep doing that," Dick advised.

"I'm getting good at it," said Tony. "Never had the guts to do that before."

"You're getting good," said Dick.

Tony got out, strode boldly to the middle and dived in; when his head appeared again he was half way down the pool. His head was like a seal's head. He attempted the breast-stroke. In a slow rhythm, his red cheeks sucking in the air and, exhaling noisily, he drew near the four.

"That's the way," said Dick, "slowly but surely, keep it up!"

Tony didn't stop when he reached the shallow end. He continued swimming, until he reached the railings and pulled himself out.

"That's the way to do it," he said, panting with satisfaction. "See that?"

His chest expanded. He gave his paunch a few resounding slaps.

"I'll have to get rid of this," he said.

"I could do that ten times over without a break," he said, "and if I could get rid of this I could do it all day. Sure, ye'll never learn at all," he said.

He commenced again, making for the deep end, snorting like a walrus.

"Ye'll never get the hang of it," he said.

He was churning the water. Dick told him to go easy. Not to be exhausting all his energy.

"Like that lot below you mean?" he said, sarcastically.

"I'm getting better every day," he said.

"You are," affirmed Dick.

"That lot there are drownin'," said Tony.

"They're o.k.," said Dick.

"Let's go down and give 'em some helpful advice," suggested Tony.

"Let's not get involved," said Dick.

"Why aren't you all out workin'?" thundered Tony. "On a fine day like this and the sun beamin' down from the heavens and here you are in the pool. Have you no shame? Wouldn't you be better off out walkin' if you've nothing else to do? It's much healthier to be outside and that's where I'm goin' to be soon!"

Tony suddenly grabbed the man's leg. He lost his balance and went under. Limbs flailing until Tony released him. It took a while for him to catch his breath and recover his composure.

"I wouldn't let you drown," said Tony. "I'm here to save you. If you can't put your head in the water, how do you expect to be able to swim?"

The man had swallowed water. He was coughing and visibly angry.

"There isn't a foot of water there," said Tony. "You're a gas man."

"And you're a creep!" said the other.

"It's always best to keep a cool head," said Tony.

He called to Dick.

"You come up here," said Dick.

"Watch me," said Tony to the 'monk'. He dived into the shallow water. He lay on his belly at the bottom of the pool and remained there for a while.

"That requires an effort," he said. "The water will bring you up if you let it."

He dived in again, his two hands on the bottom and his legs rising perpendicularly in the air.

"That, too, requires effort," he announced.

"I'll do it again and you count!" he said.

"Now you try!"

The other said that he had had enough for one day.

"Ah, you'll never learn," said Tony. "Look at me again!"

"I'm in a bit of a hurry," said the man.

"What's your rush? You'll learn from me if you just listen. But leave the bubble-bubble toil and trouble gang behind you. Come with us. You'll never learn anything if you're with them. I'll teach you how to swim. What did you say your name was?"

*   *   *

The sun shone brightly on high. Tony walked, leaving the city behind him. He regularly took long walks. It put in the day and it was a healthy pastime. He regretted, however, that it seemed to have little effect on his pot-belly. The length of the walk would depend on what company he would meet. If the company was right and they had time on their hands, he mightn't leave the city at all.

He had different walks mapped out in his head, of different lengths and varying scenery. Two-mile, five-mile and ten-mile walks. He knew exactly how long from A to B and B to C. Every morning, come hail or sunshine, he'd get up early.

He had reason to rise with the sun. For some time now he had another purpose in life, a mission that increased his zest and ambition, renewed his life as a person and as a man, bestowing on him a portion of dignity and hope which had made him an important human being. Consequently, he could hold his head higher, his step had vigour, he could face the world and his fellow creatures on earth with more confidence. His mission was clearest during bad weather, though accidents could happen as well during good spells. He continued redoubtedly, on his guard each day, each evening, each night.

He was naked apart from shorts and shoes. He would take the sun and the heat as long as they lasted, and the fresh air. Since he had the opportunity, why not go for it?

"Hi ya buddy!"

Tony's hand was raised in greeting. While his 'buddy' replied cheerfully he showed no inclination to make conversation.

"Wretch!" shouted Tony. "Dung-bettle! Who does he think he is?"

He regretted having greeted him so airily. He wouldn't do it again.

"Mangy shite," roared Tony. "Let him take a flyin' fuck for himself."

He'd been told that it was important to greet people in a friendly manner, that it would lead to a friendly reply, to chat, stand awhile and talk. He believed it. But everyone wasn't nice. Few people were nice. Like your man, plenty of time and free as a bird, but stuck up; not worth bothering with. Such people turned his stomach.

"That's what he'll do now," Tony said to himself. "He'll walk to the river, sit on a bench and to keep his arse happy he'll take out his wallet, put it on the bench and sit on it."

"Bastard," shouted Tony. "He wouldn't give a present to God or man. Let him keep his presents!"

Throw him into the river, that what's Tony would like to do. Creep up behind him and topple himself and the bench into the river. Stand on the bank, watching. The miserly whore, he'd die first before offering peace-money. Keep your money, you whore you.

There was a bull in the field. If he had been there before, Tony had never seen him. He knew the field well. Bullocks and inferior heifers grazed there. But this great big animal was a bull, accompanied by a herd of cows. The bull was keeping his eye on them.

Tony went down to the fence and began shouting to the bull. The bull was stuffing himself with grass and paid no attention at all to Tony, apart from a haughty glance. Tony continued with his antics. Was there a special way to call a bull? If he had a red rag? Offer him a handful of grass maybe? What a stubborn bastard he was. Go into the field? Could be risky. He continued to goad the bull.

"*Hurrish*! *Hurrish*! you devil!" Though he knew that *hurrish* only worked on pigs.

"*Hoirt*! *Hoirt*!"

That was to tell cattle to go on. How could he madden that bull, provoke him to come over? There and then he sent a stone spinning across the field. He hit his mark but all the bull did was to move further from him.

"Cowardy cowardy custard!"

He went over to another fence, closer to the bull. What a big fellow! The bulk of him! The weight of him, compared to the bullocks. What a devilish destruction is castration. The bullocks, poor things, so fragile beside him, beside this fine noble beast, that you'd hardly notice them.

Tony looked at the scrotum between the bull's legs. It was epic, something out of the *Táin*.

He started egging the bull again, acting the clown by the fence. The bull looked at him. Tony looked back. What a forehead, white and curly. The prominent, moist nose with drops on it. Large, heavy, loose-limbed body, rippling with muscles. A bit like himself, thought Tony. His own pot-belly was no more than a girth. He went down on his hands and feet. Such fine vigorous limbs he had, choice sinews, perfect muscles. Super limbs, his arms and legs. A fine sturdy neck, like the bull. He flexed his muscles and felt on top of the world. Would he be able to take on the bull? Would he win? Say a child was in the field and the bull attacked, would he be able to save the child? Wouldn't that be something! A medal for bravery and his photo in the papers maybe. In the event of an attack, how could someone escape if there wasn't a tree or a drain nearby? He'd have to depend on the speed of his legs. How fast would the bull be? He'd lunge, slowly at first; picking up speed he'd be hard to stop. He'd be like a tank. Would he be able to stand in front of him, jump to the side at the last second, the bull thundering past him, grab him by the neck maybe and twist it?

Grab him by the horn, or the nose, and knock him suddenly to the ground?

Tony stared at the scrotum. An epic, no less, the lower half full, slender at the top; pendulous. Maybe that was the best way to tame this creature: give him the boot, fairly and squarely, in the jewels? A good kick with hob-nailed boots and those jewels would be devalued quickly. Tony imagined the pitiful wailing of the bull, stumbling painfully through the field. But there's the rub: how to get a good kick at him. Such a kick would rid him of his bullishness in an instant, he thought. He would dearly love to try it now,

just to see. If he could get a good long stick, or hit his mark
with a stone?

*   *   *

Tony heard the railings of the new bridge in the distance
whistling. A sign of wind, a southeasterly. A lot of people
complained about the whistling bridge but he rather liked
it. It was company. He'd often lie in bed listening to it as
the curlews made their way to the north. These querulous
people agitated him. They were organising themselves to
lobby the Corporation to do something. They were
supposed to put some type of netting on the railings, it had
worked in Britain, or so they said. He hoped it wouldn't
work here. He needed that music in his ears and would be
lonesome without it. Couldn't you call it 'The Musical
Bridge' and tourists could come to see it? He wanted to call
it 'Curlew Bridge' when suggestions for its name were
requested but his notion was given short shrift. He wrote a
letter to the local paper, proposing that name, but nobody
was impressed. It was called 'Riverbridge' – hardly
original. What could be more native than the curlew? If
people knew their history, they'd know the city was built on
a fen. No shame in that. 'Curlew Bridge'? It would be
recognition, of sorts, for the dispossessed birds.

He got up, got dressed and prepared himself smartly for
the day, like other days. He brought a rope with him. He
walked the street with a vibrancy in his step, stepping out
like never before. That's the advantage of cold weather, the
air is invigorating. He liked the cold. He enjoyed
disagreeing with folks about the weather. They wondered
at him going out at all in the inclement weather.

"Tony, isn't it early you're up and about!" Thinking
he'd rather be under the blankets.

"If only I could be like you. Why so early? Isn't the day long enough?"

They really pissed him off. Denigrating the weather if there wasn't some heat in it. Basking bloody newts! Coolness is what warmed his bones.

He walked towards the river and wandered along its banks. He'd prefer the music from the bridge to be more distinct and more pitiful. That's when he most enjoyed it, loudly wailing, filling the air and eddying in the vortex of gusts, bringing the banshee with it and all the keening women of the skies. It wasn't such a day. He stood on the bridge and faced into the wind that tussled his mop of hair. Blowing into his face. He resisted its force. That wasn't difficult today. He liked to face the wind on a gusty day. The river was in flood. Those few who were out were hurrying somewhere. What was their hurry? Hurrying to work or hurrying home from the weather? And what was his hurry? More urgent, perhaps, than theirs?

He would walk a part of the river bank. Out into the country. As he proceeded, the river would become wider, the weather more blustry, the water rougher, the place more dangerous. On a really wild day that place out there with its sheer cliffs and deep ravines could be very dangerous. The sea-birds, even, would leave their cliff-ledge homes and come inland for shelter when it turned bad. But that was when he would feel in top form, his gala day.

On the river-docks stood a great heap of wooden poles. Piled there waiting for the big boats to take them to another country. They would be cut into boards aboard, or pulped for paper. Some of the boards and some of the paper would return, it was said. Why couldn't the boards and the paper be made at home, thus creating employment? He wasn't the only person to ask this question. How often had he looked for a job? The answers he got. The hangmen, the politicians, sitting comfortably on their arses, up in the Dáil with precious little to do except draw a fat salary and expenses, every single good-for-nothing one of them. He failed to see how the public could vote for such a shower that were incapable of running the country, of dividing the country's wealth equitably, creating jobs, demanding proper working conditions. He had little confidence in the electorate. People had become too soft, they had been hoodwinked. Worst thing that ever happened to the country was the proliferation of television channels; the populace had become couch potatoes, zapping away from one programme to the next. That's all they did, that's all they wanted to do, that's all they were capable of. In front of the box, from morning to night. No desire to work, to protest. If they had some other pastime, kick a ball or go for a walk. People were too well off, they had everything on the plate for them, and that's the way the Government desired it so that revolution would be imponderable.

*   *   *

"How's it going buddy?"

Tony dashed across the street to Liam, grinning from ear to ear.

"How's she cuttin' friend?"

"Oh, hi," says Liam, clearly taken aback. Tony, once again, was sporting the minimum of wear – shorts, canvas shoes and stockings. A bronzed hulk as ever, pot-bellied.

"You haven't been swimmin' since," said Tony.

"I haven't," answered Liam.

"I go every day," said Tony.

"You're good," said Liam.

"You could be just as good," said Tony.

"The other fella helps you," said Liam.

"Between ourselves that little fart helps nobody but himself," said Tony. "I was able to swim before he learned to float in his mothers womb. I used to work on the oil-rigs in the North Sea. And that's what it was – work. I'd swim in the sea there. Cold? You bet, riddled with whales and sharks and what not. I'd jump in all the same."

"Why wouldn't you!" said Liam

"You can be sure, and it's not blowin' my own trumpet I am or anythin' . . ." said Tony.

"Oh, don't I know . . ." said Liam.

". . . and that's the truth!" said Tony.

"Of course," said Liam.

"Won a medal . . ." said Tony.

"You did," said Liam.

" . . . not tryin' to blow my own trumpet now or anything . . ."

"Don't I know that!"

"I'll tell you somethin' now," said Tony.

"Go on," said Liam.

" . . . your man Dick is only a piss-artist," said Tony.

"Are you serious?" said Liam

"And I wouldn't even piss on him," said Tony.

"Japers . . ." said Liam.

"You might think I'm an old fella . . ." said Tony.

"No way!" said Liam.

" . . . well, before we go, and the two of us are in a bit of a rush, what age do you think I am?" asked Tony.

"Oh, sure you're a young man yet," said Liam.

"I'm forty years of age and they think out in the Raheen estate that I'm past it as they say," said Tony.

"No way boy!"

"I was on the dole this twenty years. They give me all sorts of excuses. I keep myself well, take a walk everyday, go for a swim as you've seen yourself, I'm a fit man but those shitheads they won't even listen to you . . ."

"Fuck the whole lot of them," said Liam.

"Now you've said it, the whole lot of them, right up to

their full bellies," said Tony. "I keep myself well, three healthy meals per day, none of your greasy sausages, rashers or black puddin' for me, never bother with the frying pan – all that stuff would kill a horse, not to mind a man; I see the other lodgers, the cut of them, younger than me but fatsos all of them, balloons, get up in the morning and all they do is go to bed again at night, haunted by the fry – sometimes it's swimmin' in grease, turn your stomach it would, but that's how they are, can't stand being under the same roof with them, but I've my own room, thank heaven . . ."

"Thanks be to the Lord Jesus," said Liam.

"And to his Blessed Mother. Never stay on there except I had me own room, I'm tellin' you, I'd be off and they could stick their flat up a donkey's arse. I've my own room and I keep the door shut and locked. I'll tell you now how I spend my day, I know you're in a bit of a hurry, I don't get much of a chance to talk with refined folk like yourself, and I won't keep you a minute, I get up in the morning I do, wash myself and go down to the kitchen, make myself a big breakfast, the other buckos waiting for the landlady to make it for them, I make my own and I'm away, away to Raheen and back again and then I meet up with Dick and we're off to the swimmin' pool. Go back to the digs then and have my dinner and after my dinner I'm off again, I've my own job, and I walk till it's evenin'. I stay out till it's late and back to the digs for ten. Never touch drugs or alcohol. I've a few horses and I give 'em a feed of grass. Out to the shop for a video, watch it in my room and then have a look at the paper."

"What horses are these?" asked Liam.

"Show horses."

"Your own!"

"What else?"

"Where do you have 'em?"

"In the garden."

"You're right to avoid the pub anyway . . .'

"Wouldn't darken the door, or if I did 'twould be only for a mineral."

"You're a good man . . . "

"I'll tell you why I don't drink. There was a time I drank a lot. I was an alcoholic. I'd be off to the boozer and drink it dry and that wouldn't be enough by half because I'd be off to another one then, and then another. I'll tell you what saved me from the drink: swimmin'! I started swimmin'. That took me out of the bad company."

Tony grinned broadly and stared straight at Liam.

"Bit of a quare one, eh? Strange the way things happen. I've one great desire in life, and that's to save someone's life. I'd give anythin' to save someone's life. Anyone. Heard a story on the radio the other day about someone being killed. Said to myself if only I'd been there. Save someone's life. That's no joke, that's an act of heroism I'd say, would you agree? You could be awarded a medal for savin' someone's life. I'd love to be able to save someone's life!"

"Be great!" said Liam.

"I'm tellin' you, wouldn't it?" said Tony.

"It sure would," said Liam.

"What would be the best way, I wonder?" asked Tony.

"Oh, couldn't say really," said Liam.

"I often think of it," said Tony.

"It's no wonder," said Liam.

"Saw someone drownin' once," said Tony, "not a pretty sight, saw him surfacin' the second and third time. He never came up again. There was nothin' I could do and I tell you I wasn't very proud of myself."

"I'm sure you weren't," said Liam.

"Used to be scared of water then," said Tony.

"Did you say 'twas a man or a woman?" asked Liam.

"Actually I think 'twas a woman. Yes, it was," said Tony.

"Dear God," said Liam.

"Do you know they take ten bodies a week out of that river?" said Tony

"I didn't know that!" said Liam.

"They do. I see the guards at it," said Tony.

"Where?" said Liam.

"Everywhere," said Tony.

"Where mostly?" asked Liam.

"The institute below is one of the worst in the country sure," said Tony. "They call it a furnace. This country's the worst in the world for it!"

"I see the guards pullin' them in, hardly recognisable, eery colour, some of them would have been a long time in the water," said Tony.

"Would they?" said Liam.

"I walk by the bank of the river, searchin'," said Tony.

"When?" asked Liam.

"All the time," replied Tony.

"What day?" asked Liam.

"If you saved yourself would it be as heroic as savin' someone else?" asked Tony.

"That's a sixty-four-thousand-dollar-question, we'll meet again with the help of God," said Liam.

"And His Holy Mother," said Tony.

"You might teach me how to swim?" said Liam.

"We might teach each other," said Tony.

"Would you have a drink?" asked Liam.

When he stood on the rail of the bridge and faced the wind it nearly choked Tony, nearly tearing the mop of hair clean off his head. The song of the bridge was playing in his head and resounding out over the city. No part of the city was untouched by its jingle. And he was at its centre, the jingle swelling, humming, howling like a gathering of keening women wailing in unison as one gigantic banshee. The water in the river was cold and sullen, full of eddies and treacherous currents.

Tony left the bridge and walked on, holding a coil of rope in his left hand. He strode forcefully along the path, the surface made easier by sand and tar, alders fencing it off from the wind, but he saw few people. Not even a dog. The beasts of the field taking shelter from the wind.

The path grew narrower, the ground more uneven. The wind carrying drops of rain. The water of the river, parallel to him racing past him to the east, the choppy waves like cavalry at full gallop. The singing of the bridge getting fainter and fainter. He scrutinised the bank as closely as he could.

When he passed the Head he was in the teeth of the gale blowing from the Atlantic. The path was narrow and crooked from here on. Up, down, up and down again but gradually rising. There was mud on the path. It was slimy and slippery, with pools of trapped water. Here and there a rockfall had partly covered it. The path led to the cliff, to the centre of the cliff, half way up, half way down the in and out. The cliff below him and above him. The sea roared below. It roared incessantly. The white horses of the sea were visible, stretching the breadth of the ocean. Now and again Tony heard what sounded like a panting animal near him, a wild dog leaping and bounding down the cliff's edge ready to pounce on him. Now and again he heard something beside him like the purr of a cat. The sea's eternal crying was making him dizzy.

He made his way up. When he reached his destination, the top of the cliff, he was terrified and totally distracted. Panting and drenched to the skin, from rain and perspiration. He rested against a rock and, leaning over, looked down. The creek fissure-like, far below, the riptide making its way through it, inland. It had come as far as below where he stood, in and out, snarling, whining like a crazed one. He was perspiring heavily. Tony thought he heard voices. He listened and now thought he could hear them clearly. Human voices. Screams, howls, sickening entreaties.

"Save me," they were saying.

"Save me, save us!"

The sea bellowed wildly.

"Where are ye? Where are ye?" Tony roared.

"We're drowning, drowning, drowning!"

"We're here, here, here!"

He ran here and there frantically.

"I'm here!"

The Snowman

He got up from his knees, put out the light and climbed on to the bed that stretched close to the wall along the window. On his knees again, on the bed, he looked out at the night outside, the darkness, the shrouded countryside, the lamps. Which houses had lamps? Were there stars in the sky, myriads of stars? A great yellow moon? He might hear a dog bark. He did. You didn't have to put out the lights in the room to hear the dogs but you did to see the lights. He loved looking out, imagining who was still awake, who had gone to bed. This ritual extended the day that little bit extra.

He startled. It wasn't the night, the darkness or the lamps that astounded him but the falling flakes. At first he didn't quite grasp what was happening. That it was snow. It was snowing!

He leaped from the bed and dressed hurriedly. He put on a pair of slippers. Down the stairs he flew.

"It's snowing!" he cried feverishly. "I'm going out for a while!"

He wanted to get out before being restrained. Maybe they hadn't heard him. Maybe the television was too loud.

Big white flakes falling, falling; like confetti swirling in the air or bits of paper dropped from an aeroplane. Thousands of them, millions. Softly falling in graceful silence. Down from the vaults of heaven. He looked up. Gently falling on his face, falling on his eyes. On his eyelashes. Falling on his mouth, cheeks, chin. Ever so tenderly. They melted. He caught them in his fist. The warmth of his skin turned them to water. Metamorphosing the dark land. All becoming white. Not yet a covering, but the groundwork had begun. By morning the miracle would be complete, he hoped.

Who opened the door? Who's there? Who called? His mother yelled at him when she saw him outside.

"Óban!" she cried.

She ordered him in at once. The young boy became frisky. He started to gad about.

"Óban!" she cried again.

She had seen this carry-on before, intoxicated by play, drunk with joy, like some half-wit. For a child who was normally so docile she sometimes believed his erratic behaviour signified some weakness, a mental aberration. You wouldn't know what to make of him sometimes. Sudden fits of uncontrollable glee or bouts of sheer pique. Salivating at the mouth at times with unmitigated joy, like a year old babe, pleasure gurgling in his throat. And then boiling with rage, or in a deep sulk, totally impenetrable like a dog protecting a bone. Ten years old now. Was it because he was an only child?

Out she went to grab him. He escaped. Off he goes as frisky as a colt, kicking his heels. Beaming with laughter. Merriment resounding from him. His mother grew cross.

"Wait there till I get the stick!" says she. "Come in!" says she.

She said she wouldn't go trapsing after him and not to think she would, whatever the fool he was.

But she did catch hold of him and dragged him in after her. She shook him. Whatever class of a buffoon was he?

"Now do you see yourself," says she. "Do you see the cut of you? Not a shoe on you. Look at the state of your slippers!"

She smacked his backside.

"Look at your clothes!" says she. "Do you think I've nothing better to be doing than to be running after you? Do you see your hair? Throw those clothes off you," she ordered. "Have I nothing better to do than to be getting dry clothes and pyjamas for you?"

He must be chilled to the bone, she thought. They said boys don't catch a cold, but that's nonsense. Why wouldn't they? Many a boy caught pneumonia. She ordered him upstairs to take a bath and not to be thinking she'd do that for him as well.

He was glad he could bathe alone. If there was enough water – and he'd feel the tank first – he'd send it spouting into the tub as he'd seen his father do. That's something his mother would never do. She'd only take a shower, being sparing with the water. His father would fill it so you could swim in it if the tub were bigger. He often envied his father in all that water, like a playful walrus. That's what he wanted, to splash and cavort in the soft water. On his back and on his stomach and stretching out fully. A fish in water. Water, water, everywhere. He looked forward to it, now that he had to wash his hair as well. He'd baptise himself with water, allowing it to flow down over him. He'd fill the big blue sponge and disgorge the water over him, again and again. He'd have plenty of foam and would remain there, playing, until the water became cool.

He sat in front of the mirror, drying his mop of hair. The new drier was much better than the old one. Stronger, a gust of wind blowing through his hair. They'd bought quite a few gadgets recently. Look how white the skin is on the crown of his head. But not the white of snow.

Oh the snow. Always coupled with Christmas in his mind. Always expecting snow for Christmas, but it rarely fell on time. Now Christmas was over and it would be an eternity before it came round again. People said snow comes mostly in January or February. Those months, too, were gone. It had been very mild this year: grass coming up, flowers coming out. The crocus blossomed, daffodils and primroses in the beds opposite the house, his mother sprinkling poison from a bottle to keep the slugs and pests away from the new growth. He saw the 'pookies' stretched out dead in the morning like slime on the earth. They were saying it might snow yet, that it often snowed in March, April, even into May. They were right. It was March and the snow was coming down. There are places where it is always snowing, in the North Pole and in the South Pole. He found it hard to imagine snow in the South Pole. He associated it with heat. South means heat, France, Spain, Italy, Africa. But he learned at school that the South Pole has as much ice and snow as the North, since each was equidistant from the sun. He also learned of other areas that are snow-covered permanently, that snow remains on high peaks. At first he thought that was odd, since these peaks had to be nearer the sun than anywhere else on earth. But he was told that high peaks are always cold and he saw himself that this was true. Snow could often be seen where Granny lived, patches of snow here and there in mountainy crevices.

His mother came upstairs and asked him was he ready. She brought him warm pyjamas from the hot press. They felt wonderful, fresh, warm, comfortable. She ordered him back to bed, warning him not to turn on the radio. To go straight to sleep. She shoved him under the bed-clothes, kissed him on the top of the head and told him to say his prayers.

"I've said them!"

She said he could say a few more. He had no intention of doing so but he did intend to look out once more at the snow. All the snow in heaven was falling. Thanks be to God! He turned on the radio and got under the blankets again He loved music even when barely audible. With the help of music it was easy to lie under the bedclothes, stretched comfortably. Nice thoughts would come to him then. And it was easy to switch it off if he heard his mother approaching. Unless he fell asleep. His mother often complained that the radio was left on, that she was always turning it off. But her bark was worse than her bite. It was she herself who gave him the radio and allowed him to have it in the room when they bought a new one. The new one could play cassettes and was much better than the Hi-Fi they had in the sitting room. It could even play records.

He hoped the snow would become even denser. Let it fall, fall and cover the house. Let them be snow-bound inside. Not able to go to school or even to the shop. There were places where snow was up to the height of a house, a two-storey house, where snow piled up relentlessly. Where Granny lived, snow often covered the sheep in the hills during the depth of winter. Snow driving its way into their sheltered nooks. They would lie in the snow until it melted or until they were rescued. You'd know where they were from the breathing holes in the snow. If you saw a huge sieve of holes you'd know the whole flock was buried together. The warmth of their breath creating the holes as the snow piled on them. If it didn't go on too long they'd be none the worse after it.

Though his Granny's house was not as comfortable as his own he liked it, especially in summer. They didn't spend much time there in winter. His mother was always giving out how cold it was there, doors and windows open all the time and when they weren't you could still feel draughts coming through the joints. But he liked the big open hearth and the turf-fire. Sitting by the fire at night. The floors were of concrete though rugs were placed near the beds. Is wasn't only his mother who felt the cold. He always had goose-pimples and if it weren't for the hot water bottle Granny gave him he'd be frozen.

He liked his Granny, though she was very old, stooped and bedraggled. She was constantly knitting pullovers for him and giving him tasty morsels to eat, a fistful of coins and always praising him and remarking how clever he was. His mother too would say he was clever, and he believed he was. Didn't he know everything about the ozone layer and the destruction of the rain forests in Brazil, acres of trees felled in one hour – the size of three thousand football pitches. And not only in Brazil, but all over the Tropics, in Africa, India, Australia and elsewhere. He had read in the paper that scientists were predicting great climatic changes, that the fine weather would come in winter and vice versa. There would be massive earthquakes in places where they had never previously occured, many animals, fish and birds would be doomed. He wouldn't like that to happen, snow falling in summer.

*   *   *

A sheet of white snow. Piled up against the window panes. The plots beyond the lawn, white, as white as the lawn itself. Hills, valleys, glens. The mountain. Each ditch snow-hooded. Every bush under a weight of snow, every branch and limb. Snow on every bramble. Every tree in the coniferous wood a pale sentry.

Over all things a peaceful white reigned supreme. River banks, right down to the water, completely white. The river itself a greyish torpor. Every roof crowned with snow. Only a few remaining areas of shade where the snow had not yet blown in. He looked out at the blanched countryside, as giddy as a child opening a present under the Christmas tree.

He appeared at the door of the house, well fitted out in high rubber boots, overcoat and a scarf around his neck. He had gloves on and a knitted leprechaun cap on his head, covering his ears. Suddenly he picked up a handful of snow and made a snowball. When he threw it out on the snowy lawn a red-breasted bird flew across to the little stone wall. But he hardly noticed it.

There was enough snow to make thousands of snowballs to throw at targets. He went out to the middle of the lawn, the snow crunching underfoot. The traces of his boots remained in the bright deep carpet.

He was going to make a big snowman, the biggest ever built; it would stand like a white giant on the side of the hill and be a source of wonder to all who'd see him, from the road or from further afield.

He began to mould and squeeze the snow. What fun, with so much snow. This great big lump was only the beginning, he'd add to him. Making him the king of all snowmen. The greatest that ever was built.

He discarded his gloves as they had got too wet. Were it not for his mother he wouldn't bother with them at all. The snow felt different in his bare hands. Much nicer. Now he could sense its texture properly. He piled the snow, packing it densely. It was easier now with his bare hands. The grass was becoming visible. Maybe he'd use up all the snow on the lawn. And fetch more. There was no lack of snow about. But his hands were cold. His fingers tingling. Now and again he would squeeze them, shrink them, to bring back the circulation. He was getting tired as well. His back was stiff. But he wouldn't submit. He'd go on slaving. He'd see it through. He'd continue to collect the snow, to pile it on and pack it firmly. The more he worked the better he became. He learned how to roll it, to allow it to form a ball – a rolling mass.

His hands grew leathery. They hurt. Could he stand the pain much longer? Should he go in and warm them? It was hard work. The joy of it was running out.

He could barely open the door of the house. He was wheezing and panting. Whimpering. He went into the kitchen, almost whining. His mother wasn't there. She was still in bed. How long would the pain last? What should he do? He tried turning on the hot tap. He breathed on his fingers, knitting and kneading them as much as he could. The pain would eventually go – but when?

He placed the head on the snowman. He fixed the hands. He put a hat on the head. Eyes, a mouth and a nose. Black buttons down the front, from the neck to the belly-button. A pipe in his mouth and gloves on the hands. The harder he worked the more oblivious he became to everything else except the snowman. And now it was finished. The numbness in his fingers returned.

He went upstairs. His mother was getting up.

"I made a snowman!" he told her. He wouldn't say anything else until she saw its magnitude with her own eyes.

"Like to see it?" he asked.

He drew back the curtains. She saw the murky sky. A dark threatening sky. Bulging with great leaden clouds. There would be another fall. Already the odd flake was careering down.

"What do you think of it?" he asked.

Hurly Burly

I'd buy a newspaper. I'd buy *The Irish Times*. Get some info on the World Cup and Gaelic games results from home. But do you think they'd have *The Irish Times* in France? Be in French if they did. What did the French care for Gaelic games? Feck all.

Mother of Jesus, I'm a right one I am. Look at me now. Friggin' eedjit. What was I thinking of at all that I kept going on; didn't I know well there was no room, couldn't any fool see that. Edging the car forward and no place to go. Beside the traffic lights of all places. I'd squeeze into that little corner on the right, I said to myself, so my car won't get a bump. Here in the middle of the road, obstructing another car. They can stay there, may the devil shit on them! I wouldn't look at the other car or who was in her; as soon as the lights changed we'd be off and never see each other again.

Slyly, I took a peek at the opposition. And who would it be but Mrs. Boylan and her stone-faced man. Sure what was he only a lamb – he'd bleat before he'd say anything unkind. They were waving to me. Friendly, very friendly, no bother at all on them. No, these were not my foes; I had been forgiven. But they knew me, of course. She, Mrs. Boylan, was teaching in the same school as my wife.

"Hello there!"

Going out to the woods more than likely, or coming back. They liked to stroll in the mountainy woods, as did I.

The lights changed. We were off. I caught a glimpse of the other car in the mirror, turning down left and into the driveway of a house on the corner. That wasn't the Boylan's house. They entered by a wall. They didn't bother with the gate. The wooden gate was closed. Not a scratch on the car. Hold on, that wasn't the Boylans at all, or their car.

It's Pat Wallace. No one in the car but himself. Out he gets, pissed as a lord, in a lather of sweat.

"Who won the World Cup, Pat?"

"Who won the Munster Final, Cork or Kerry?"

"Kerry by about 20 points."

"Thought as much. Sure there's no other team in Munster besides Kerry. What about Connacht?"

"Mayo again!"

"Well fuck Galway, and fuck Kerry!"

"*Voulez-vous le voir?*"

"*Peut-être demain!*"

"*Voulez-vous manger?*"

"*Peut-être demain!*"

"*Peut-être demain!*" I burst out laughing. Linguaphone course, ha-ha! "Are you going to get married?" "*Peut-être demain* – weather permitting!"

"What do you expect from Galway? The rogues! Same team this past twenty years. All they're doing is resurrecting Lazaruses. They wouldn't beat Kerry now, just like the year before, they didn't get any of the action, beaten into the ground."

Hell's bells, the bridge is down. Shite and garlic! Wouldn't stay up for us, no way. And we were the next car. What luck! Holy Mary, we'll be lost in France now and not a word of the lingo. *Bonjour! Bonsoir! Comment allez-vous? Ça va? C'est tout! C'est ça? Au plaisir! À tout à l'heure! C'est très gentil a vous! Vous êtes très sympathique! A votre santè! Peut-être demain.* Ha-ha!

If I made a dash for the river at a hundred mile an hour, hundred and fifty – would the car glide over the water? She wouldn't. We'd sink like a stone. The humidity in France will be the death of us. We're half dead as it is. The spray – that was the hindleg of the devil altogether. It's not flies it's killing but the children. Aren't they gasping for breath? And our own tongues hanging out . . . it's smothered we are. Oh, for a soft day in Ireland. Look at the newspapers in a heap. Would they have *The Times*? Thought I saw it a second ago. Where did it vanish to? Didn't I see the masthead clearly. Smothered. Ruffians the whole lot of them, and all in a mad hurry. Just look at those groping hands. Only the half of it left – the second half. Did *The Irish Times* have two halves? Can't recall it did, though some papers have. Well, it must have come in two halves today. I paid 30 pence.

"Have you got *The Irish Times* my good man?"

"They're late. Call in this evening if you're in town."

I'd take the second half. Might be something in it about the matches. But the sports section was the section missing. Maybe today it would be different. A sign of luck. Must be a sign of luck. Should I ask for my 30 pence back until I return later in the evening?

Peut-être demain! Pas mal! N'importe! D'accord? À le vôtre! The one that bought the sweets was in a tizzy, giving hell to the shopkeeper. Was she given inferior sweets? The middle eaten out of them! Did you ever come across such chicanery! Is it any wonder he had only one section of *The Times*. A hundred per cent profit he wanted: thirty pence for one section and thirty again for the other. The women were backing up the customer. All women are the same. They all become viragos. Nothing at all can satisfy them now.

There was a man in the shop. He was neutral. Standing by himself to one side. Would he take the side of the women or the shopkeeper if he spoke up? He must have been fed up with the Amazonians. I'd call back again for the second half. But I was going home, this was Dublin.

I'd walk to the car. Maybe it's ready. The shopping

nearly fell out of the bag. It will surely fall out, the bag is torn. It's a wonder that it hasn't spewed all over the place already, the state the bag is in. I need a new bag. This one's old. It was already ten years old when I started to work. Bad plastic. Plastic bags are useless. Dunnes Stores plastic bags had a short life spell.

I'd take a short cut to the school where my car was parked. Best shortcut was to go into a house and out the other. Heck, this is my brother Andy's house, strange I didn't recognise it. I didn't know he was in these parts. Lift the latch and there I am, in my brother's house. Of all houses. I didn't like this particular brother, we never got on; I wouldn't stay, in the back, out the front. As they were all upstairs I wouldn't be seen. My finger on the latch of the front door, on my way out, when I heard someone coming down the stairs. I'd have to move fast. But maybe they'd see me going. Recognise me perhaps. They didn't know I was in Dublin, they wouldn't think it was me at all. How would they? I didn't know myself. I'll stay a moment.

"Sit down!"

I sat on a couch. A grand comfortable couch. Andy was well off. An architect, plenty of money stashed away. Suddenly, who should walk in but Beartla, the other brother. He strode confidently into the room, as though at home. I was taken aback. None of these two brothers got on with the other. They'd greet each other but little else. You'd rarely see them together, though they lived within a stone's throw of each other. At least I knew they lived close to each other, but not this close.

The brother – Andy, that is, the architect – was entering a competition announced in *The Connaught Tribune* for the best pint of milk. What a farce, how childish of him, a well-off city architect bothering with some petty local competition. Why couldn't he leave it to some country yokel who never left home? Where would he get the milk anyway? Oh, I forgot . . . hadn't he bought a cow, or halfbought her, and let her out into the briar field. A Jersey cow. To be sure. Hadn't I heard the rumour in a dream. The Jerseys were the best. He'd a half a pint of milk in a cardboard box, showing it to Beartla, myself getting a glimpse of it from where I was sitting, and the boasting and wonderment out of him on account of the fine fat cream on it. He himself had milked the cow. He had taken this initiative all by himself.

What harm was it to have this little hobby, the other brother wasn't a bit surprised – the brother that came in, the soldier not the architect – that he should be entering for competitions. He alway entered a sod for the annual competition for newly-cut turf. But he wasn't an architect but a soldier and part-time farmer. He was meant to be a farmer but he didn't stay on the farm; off he goes and joins the army. When all was said and done it was nice to be entering for competitions back home for old time's sake.

What's this? Beartla sitting down to a meal? They're feeding him and never asked me had I a mouth on me. Beartla lashing into the grub greedily, voraciously, as befits a soldier. He was in a hurry. So was I. How carefully they played host to Beartla, something they never did before. They'd more time for him than me and that was something new. They had time for me, once, fellow-professional . . . though maybe not all the time in the world. Andy wouldn't go overboard about anyone, being a bit stuck-up, but maybe this fuss about the competitions, the excitement, preparation and concern, had made him more gregarious.

He was eating a salad. It wasn't much of a meal. Hardly more than a handful of hay. Wouldn't satisfy a rabbit. A cheap, stringy meal. A soldier's meal, a part-time farmer's meal in a city. But it wasn't the contents of the meal but the attitude. It was the attitude I disliked. They fixed Beartla a meal in a jiffy, a busy man that shouldn't be delayed. I'd show the devils that I was no walkover, that I was a man of substance, a man in a hurry, someone not to shilly shally with.

I got up and went over to my shopping on the opposite couch, the milk, the lettuce and eggs. I took the bag and walked to the door. They made no attempt to discourage my leaving. Isn't the brother something else! They didn't try to stop me or say 'wait a while' – nothing. She herself was washing her hair and said not a word. Was it herself or her daughter? Was she upstairs all the while? They hadn't got a daughter. Was it a son? Someone was washing or drying hair.

Let them all frig off. Let them stay quiet. What do I care? When did they ever come to visit me? They'd be hopping mad but so what. I'd show them I'm not to be trifled with; I was the top dog, they'd find that out. Why didn't they try to stop me, persuade me to come back? Why didn't they say 'have something to eat, you must be starvin' – you'll have to have a bite, you will'. Why didn't they say that?

If they even offered a drop of brandy or placed the bottle in front of me. Make a fuss about me, treat me the way I deserved. Honourably. Courteously, as you'd expect. But they never said a word. Let me go without a mutter.

I was uncouth. They'd be raging at my bad manners. They'd never invite me back. Not that I had been invited.

Where did I leave the car? Did I leave her at the school and walk to the garage or did I drive to the garage? I thought I'd left her on this side of the school, her front to the slope of the yard, her back to the wall-flanked wood. I'd look the other side. They said she'd be ready, that there'd be no delay. What did I do with her? I was nearly certain I had left her at the school; on the left slope, her back to the wood-flanked wall? Or the right slope, narrow, steep, triangular. Or at the bottom of the yard below? Her nose facing the open top of the triangle but one cut in half, a straight line through the middle and half of it gone. The chunk missing was where the school stood, the wall and the structure of the school. A blue Toyota, Datsun Sunny, a car with a bit of length, an estate. God Almighty, where did I leave her?

Anne was there. Walking from her car to the school. Where'd she come from? What's she doing in Dublin? Of course, she'd said she'd be coming.

"Where's my car, Anne? Do you think I left it here or in the garage?"

Nearly sure I left it here. Wouldn't be stolen, would it? I'm always afraid my car will be stolen. Do I see her at the end of the yard? Down there at the crossroads? She must have slipped down by herself; brakes gone wrong. Always afraid of that. That the brakes might go. She's gone down the road a good bit. The way she's sticking out it's a wonder nothing rammed into her or she into something else. Not a scratch on her. How easy it is to cause havoc, to kill a child, a teacher, or a woman with her shopping basket. Get down there quick.

"Is that a blue car at all? Is she a Datsun? She's a different bonnet. This one has a sloping bonnet."

"I'll drive you, come on!"

"That's your car? What made you park her that way, sixty degrees off the road? That's a dark road, even if it's a main road, the road to Daingean, a hilly road; the way the houses have appeared there below you'd swear it was a suburb of Galway. Used to walk it long ago with my bike, young trees coming up, still in their boxes, could cause an accident."

There'd be no delay. It wasn't taking her out of her way, in and out that's all, she thought.

"Where did I leave the car Anne? Why did I come to Dublin Anne? I knew you had to come but all I wanted was a pint of oil. Couldn't I get it in Limerick? Why didn't I go with you or take the train as I usually do? Hang it, where did I leave the car? Anne where did I leave her? Talk to me. Ask me where I was. I might remember . . ."

A passenger. I'm sitting hunched up in the passenger seat. In my wife's small Golf. She's a sensitive type. Red shoes on her. And red fingernails. And a red safety belt across her black jumpsuit.

"Good girl Anne, good girl!"

An older car than mine but often livelier. Crimson-purple, the paint scraped off here and there but never a sign of rust – as was to be seen on my new one. I was feeling funny in the head. I put my hand to my head.

"Anne, speak to me."

Anne was looking straight ahead.

"Anne sweetheart, good girl!"

I placed my hand playfully on her knee. Looked sideways at her, friskily. From the corner of my eye I noticed that Anne took her left hand from the steering wheel and touched a spot between her eyebrows. She was praying.

"Anne, I'm o.k. Don't be worried."

A tear brimmed in her eye. Suddenly I felt utterly hopeless. Why couldn't I remember where I'd left the car? The sweat poured off me. I began to tremble. If Anne were to ask me – ask me where I'd been, where I stopped, where I went, where I was? Terror forced a drop from my eye.

"Anne, I'm o.k. Don't be worried!"

She burst into tears. Her cheeks were streaming.

"If you like we can pray together," she said.

Tryst

Veils of strange spirit-like mist sometimes shot through with interludes of light. The sun bidding to burst forth. It will burst forth with glittering light. Every tendril on every tree-twig, every grass-growth was laden with dewy droplets. When the sun shoots through in a while it will light up the landscape, making it gleam and sparkle, with brilliant brightness.

The sheep in the field beside the river have crystals in their fleeces. As they lie, blackfaced, they look like a gathering of monsters.

A smaller shape moves through the flock in a ramble of fits and starts. Irregular, capricious. Pausing, finally, at a bare shoulder of a trench to swivel its ears. Hares, it is said, in spite of being nocturnal feeders, dislike getting wet, even with the dew.

A larger shape follows.

Swallows and swifts begin to circle. They fly high. Two blackbirds land on the lawn, one is female.

Vèronique and Noel, hand in hand, come walking down to the river-bank, while the workers from the village in their straw hats enter the field to pick strawberries.

A teenage girl trots her pony through the woods. Up down, up down, she goes.

The shrubs growing by the river-bank are in bloom. Azalea, rhododendron, wisteria. They grow in no dilettanish order. Sparrows and finches play. Vèronique first and then Noel bend their heads to fill their senses with scent. A hawk hovers overhead. Vèronique and Noel stroll to the middle of the bridge.

She is attired in a bright dress. Her black hair is long

and flowing. Noel is dressed in a bright red shirt with jet-black denims. His hair is also crow-black but short, with a frisette. They both wear earrings.

A frog sits on a waterlily leaf.

"Look!"

They recline over the parapet of the bridge.

Noel points to a brown trout.

A kingfisher jets in underneath. Friesian cattle come down to investigate. A wood-pigeon coos in an ivied white-thorn bush. In France, watched by their peers, seated on long benches, men and women play *boule*, shaded by tall translucent trees.

"Twinkle, twinkle little star, how I love you where you are! Up above the world so high, like an angel in the sky!"

A woman cuts briars by the walls with a reaping-hook. What a beautiful yellow day, she seems to say. Her reaping-hook is the finest reaping-hook he has seen in a long time. She attacks the briars with vigour, clad in green wellingtons, her left hand clothed in a heavy glove. Her bare right hand has multiple red scratches. But she doesn't mind.

Her house, near the guest-house, nestles in blossoms. It seems to keep watch like a benevolent lord. Hens and a regal cock peck at flies and moths and mawks beside her. From time to time the cock crows. All is warm and pleasant. There is a dog and a cat there, too. The woman starts to comb her hair with the reaping-hook. I don't mind, she seems to say, I don't mind at all. They don't mind because birds sing in their hearts.

"I wonder is she really blind? It seemed to me that she saw us!"

"The character of a face does not derive from its various proportions but from the spiritual light which is reflected in it."

Fields of golden corn. Ears of barley and wheat. Cornflowers.

Cowslips. Primroses. Glistening buttercups. Bluebells. Red poppies. Speedwell and forget-me-not. Figwort and meadow-sweet. Elderberry. Brighteye. Lilac and laburnum. The white grasses of Parnassus.

Noel offers a flower to Vèronique. She hoists her head. His left hand, already embracing her body, couples her to him. Their pursed lips meet.

A Fresher

The trees were mainly beech, ash or sycamore, but there were also some lime trees. He did not know all the names but he did notice the differences in shape and in foliage, and that some of them had shed their leaves more than others. There was a tennis court at the top of the park, with a couple of women playing.

They played nonchalantly, talking and laughing as women do. Tennis was such a ghoul of a game, he thought. Though Pam looked nice in her white gear, she wasn't too thin. His Mum had wished him to play, she had joined him in a club and had sent him for tuition, but he wasn't interested. Then she insisted on him learning the piano. What a ghoul of an instrument! He liked the guitar but his Mum didn't. He liked to sing as he played, and he wrote his own songs. He liked talking to girls. But now that he was in college he might take up something. Weight-lifting, maybe, to strengthen his poor muscles. His biceps were no bigger than hen-eggs, his chest was as flat and as white as the proverbial pancake, his thighs were matchsticks. Or so he thought. Nobody had said so, but he thought so. He was glad, anyway, that he hadn't grown any taller or he would be looking like a weed in a wood. But Pam had liked him the way he was, and that was enough.

These women were pathetic. If they weren't interested why did they bother? They weren't children, so nobody had forced them to play. Parents were peculiar. He wouldn't be like that. If he had children they could play if they wanted, whatever they wished, whenever they liked; because otherwise it was no good.

He liked the hugeness of the trees, their massive trunks.

When he tried to put his arms around one of them, out of curiosity, they didn't go half-way. How huge! He looked up at it admiringly. Then he patted it.

"Hail to thee, majestic tree!"

He would invite David to the park, that sounded suspicious, and he would ask him, for a bet, if he thought his arms could circle it. David was a bit of a ghoul.

The colours of the leaves were inspiring. Pam would say they were gorgeous.

"Autumnal colours!"

He liked the sound of that adjective. The fallen leaves formed a beautiful bright mosaic. Forty shades of yellow! Why had he given up Art at school? Pam would love it here. This park would be his sanctuary.

The trees in Meelick wood were tiny by comparison: straight poles of tall conifers, most of them now felled. 'Felled' was a strange word. 'The trees are felled.' He liked the music of strange words. He searched their meaning in the dictionary, always coming across so many more, but it wasn't tedious work. His vocabulary was improving. But college was harder than he thought it would be. There were so many difficult books to read and he couldn't understand the lecturers half of the time.

"Hi! Well done! You have made it into the biggest and best University in Ireland. Let me congratulate you on your results and on your good taste in choosing this University. Welcome and congratulations!"

How amusing this college literature! Such hype!

"Let me congratulate you on securing a place in this University and on making such a fitting choice! We are immensely proud that you and more than 3,000 other first years will be enrolling with us this year. There are over 14,000 students pursuing their studies."

He had been looking forward to college, to having a good time, to having lots of friends and freedom.

"There are great times ahead of you in college, times for intellectual growth, new friendships, self-discovery and challenge."

He wondered if he was intellectual enough. Why had he taken Welsh?

"Welsh is like the remnant of an oak wood!"

Such a ghoul of a subject, really, but he liked the y's and w's.

"Welsh is a protean language!"

A sort of chameleon. Doing Welsh was somewhat weird, somewhat cool. Cool things were rather useless things. 'Cool' had a polyvalence of meaning. Useless, queer and quaint. 'Quaint', that was the word he wanted. He wanted to be able to use the right word, the right word didn't always come to him, his brain failing to supply it, but he was going to read a lot, get up early and study in the library as David did. That ghoul was always up early and gone to college. He wished his landlady would call him but his landlady was another ghoul.

She was like his Mum. His Mum disliked Pam. His Mum wouldn't even say Pam's name. It even annoyed her the 'pet' way he called her.

"She's not good enough for you, Nigel!"

Now, that annoyed him.

"There are lots of nice girls in the world! Get a girl that suits you!"

Such crap. He had the girl he wanted. What was so wrong with being happy?

"She's not your kind, Nigel!"

He told himself that it wasn't that his Mum had anything personal against Pam, it was only that she was worried about him, he being her eldest.

"You worry me, Nigel! That girl worries me!"

He wished his Mum would allow him to do the worrying.

It was amazing how dark it had got. Public parks were dangerous after dark. Faggots frequented them. What exactly was a faggot, how did a faggot look?

"More than faggots frequent woods!"

"Strange things happen at night in public parks!"

Stabbings, gang-rapes, sometimes people were left tied to trees.

"There will be music by the lake, singing and dancing, and then off to the disco . . ."

The disco was crap. The college pub was crap. Since Pam had gone to England he had been looking forward to leaving home: *'pav* city'. But there were pavs everywhere, depending on where one went. The university was full of ghouls. He wondered which were the worst: pavs or ghouls? The girls were crap.

"They haven't seen you, yet, maestro!"

'Maestro' was a word he didn't like.

"Why don't you put up a sign proclaiming that Nigel has arrived? Why don't you issue t-shirts with the slogan 'We Love Nigel' and invite all the girls to wear them?"

David was a ghoul.

"Another thing, the food in the canteen is crap!"

"In there they fart on it to keep it warm!"

"I went into the canteen and I bought a ham sandwich and I swear to God the bread was stale and the meat had a pong from it!"

David was all right because he was staying at home.

"I hate this pub! See that bouncer over there, he's disgusting, all that blubber, but nobody would dare say a thing to him!"

"I'd love to stick a pin in him to see would he leak, leak, leak!"

"Drip, drip, drip, you mean!"

"This college is like a factory, you prick!"

"I met this guy a week ago and I haven't seen him since!"

"Is he taking Welsh?"

"He's taking English!"

"Even the cornflakes are worse here than at home!"

His Mum had gone hysterical when he told her that Pam could have twins. 'Is going to have twins' is what he said.

"What?" said his Mum.

"It's in her genes!" he said.

"That waif of a girl!" she said.

"It jumps a generation!" he said.

"What jumps?" she asked. "What did I tell you about that girl? She's out to get you! Her parents are out to get you! You're never to stay in that girl's house again! Putting you in the one room! Did you ever hear the likes of it? Well, I don't think much of them! You're a good catch and that's all they're after!"

"Let me tell you something, if that girl gets pregnant don't come running to me!"

There was a church near the park. He wondered if it was still open. He couldn't make out for sure if there were lights on inside, or whether or not the lights were reflections from the street. Most churches closed early because of vandals. He did not frequent churches, but this evening he would go in, sit down and meditate. Churches were refuges, sanctuaries, like the park. The odd evening he might walk to it, now that he knew where it was.

He was never before so lonely, but he wasn't near to crying or anything. He wished he had a proper friend, he had nothing in common with David. David was the landlady's son. He wished Pam was there. She had tried to get a job in Dublin, but now he didn't know when he'd see her again. He'd like to go home but he knew he couldn't. He appeared to be away for weeks. He wondered if his friends at home had forgotten him.

He walked slowly down the hill towards his digs. The darkness was pleasant. But his thoughts continued to tumble about in his brain.

"I'm sick of my digs," he said.

"I'm cold, hungry, and lonely."

"My room is too small, my bed is lousy!"

"My landlady is afraid that a crumb will fall on her carpet, that a stain will be put on her furniture!"

He was sorry that he hadn't taken a room on campus. He was thinking of leaving. He was thinking of leaving college altogether; of seeking a job in England, maybe.

The lights were on in college. Students were still studying. How sad! But he greatly envied them. David, that ghoul, was surely still in the library. David had told him to join the societies. David's English was better than his although David wasn't studying English. David seemed to have 'big words' naturally, but somehow, and maybe it was because of this naturalness, they didn't sound so good, he thought.

The Hotel looked warm. He might look for a job there, part-time. He'd have to call in to RTÉ to see if they had any job. He was good at cameras. A lot of stuff on RTÉ was junk, they hadn't a clue. To be a film maker was what he wanted, to direct films: to act in them and script them. If only he had gone to Rathmines. They had a great time in Rathmines. If you were doing journalism in Rathmines you had to become a member of The New Film Centre, and you were out with cameras every day.

"If I was in Rathmines I'd be in my element!"

Joan wasn't. She was in Rathmines but she didn't like it. She was sorry she wasn't in UCD doing English. He was doing English to give him ideas, and Psychology to show him how to deal with people and then Welsh, because it was different. But English hadn't given him any ideas so far. If anything he had less ideas now than when he started. The way he was, he couldn't think at all, he was all muddled up. Joan was hoping to write scripts and they'd work together, using his video-camera. But Joan was now going out with James, and Gillian in UL was going out with Dermot. If he had gone to UL or Rathmines this might never have happened. It was too expensive to ring Pam. Anyway his feelings for Pam were changing. For a while he hadn't been as frightened of loosing her. She wasn't as special anymore, as magic to hold or to kiss.

"I feel like a rabbit in a strange warren!"

If he didn't go home shortly he'd have no friends. No new friends and his olds friends gone.

"Who are you?"

"You were our friend but no longer!"

"You're an interloper!"

Joan wouldn't be going home on the train at weekends, she'd be staying in Dublin with James. How he had longed for those train journeys, they had talked about them, the fun they'd have, coming and going, hours each way. They would talk about life, plan the world, discuss and analyse the future; their hours on the train would be too few. Joan didn't appear to be interested in the scripts any longer.

'*Pav* city!' People just liked to run it down. Many of them never saw it. How he'd love to walk its streets, walk along the banks of the Shannon with Joan or Gillian; viewing the white swans, the bullrushes, the tufted ducks. *Pav* city of the swans!

"I know what I am, I am a physiolater!"

"A what?"

"A physiolater!"

"What are you looking at?"

"I'm not looking at you."

"Are you calling me a liar?"

He'd like to shoot the eejits. Their *pav* accents, their *pav* haircuts. You'd recognise a *pav* anywhere.

"I'm not joking, the world would be a better place without them!"

"You think you're something!"

"All they want is trouble, to hurt someone. They want to make people suffer. They enjoy seeing people in pain! The fffing eejits!"

He'd love to go to the disco in Termites and afterwards to Friar Tuck's for chips.

He'd join a whole lot of societies. The Film Society, the Drama Society, the English Society. He'd show them. Oh, and weight-lifting. He'd show them. He'd show them who he was.

David was a dickhead. Eight A's in his Leaving and still he never stopped studying. He almost looked like a pav. He wasn't interested in music or anything. He asked him about forming a band but he said he wasn't interested. He was only interested in study and going to bed early. He went to bed around eleven o'clock. He didn't go to bed until one. His landlady was giving out to him about the electricity. He watched tv in the darkness, but even then she'd look in and say to him not to be long. Being away wasn't so great after all. 'Life is a bitch and then you die!' Whoever said that was right. *"Welcome to the great college! Life is about to unfold for you. . .!"*

"Such otiosity!"

What did 'otiosity' mean? The word had kept rolling about in his brain.

He ambled down towards his digs, only a five minute walk from the college. They had looked for digs as soon as the Leaving results came out. A sunny day, all so happy, that now appeared so long ago. They had gone to the college office and were given a list of digs on big, folded, computerized pages. They decided to have lunch in the Hotel. The meal wasn't great, the Yorkshire pudding was overbaked. Then they got out the sheets and spread them on a table in the foyer, marked the near ones and rang. Being near the college they cost a bit more. Would he favour campus accomodation? Mum thought he wouldn't feed himself. He sided with Mum. Anyway one had to come back another day and queue for the 'on campus'. He now regretted his decision.

"I knew the very minute I saw her!"

Mum paid a deposit: giving her three crisp £20 notes. It was a lot of money, and that for one week only. He thought about all the things he could buy with that amount. At least he'd get soup and a dessert for dinner, he thought.

He thought about his room at home. His spacious comfortable room. Room for his guitar, amp, and Hi-Fi. All his posters on the walls. Then, dejectedly, he remembered that he no longer had his room at home, that a UL student had now taken up lodgings there.

What happened to his posters? If he went home now he would have to share a room with his younger brother, who snored.

As he passed the houses on the avenue he took particular notice of one that was larger than the rest and had a great big French window in front. The lights were on inside and a young man, about his own age or slightly older, sat working at a table in the centre of the sitting-room. It was a big dark table: plenty of space on it. His own table was tiny, stuck up against the window. Why hadn't he drawn the curtains? The room looked lovely, comfortable and warm. Pictures hung on the walls. There was a fire blazing. A sofa lying by one wall. It was easy for that bastard to study. He wondered if he was a student, going to the same college? He turned back so as to view the room a second time.

"The lucky dick!"

Opulence. He liked the sound of the word, and it

pleased him that the operative word came so quickly to him.

"He lives in opulence, in a salubrious setting, in sartorial style!"

Phrases were becoming easier. 'Sartorial style' was, perhaps, an exaggeration. From what he could glean, his dress was casual. He would surely met this fellow some day, and maybe get to know him. He had plenty of space for his tapes and CDs.

"The lucky git!"

His digs were shrouded in darkness. His landlady and her husband were probably indolently watching tv in their own luxurious sitting-room. He wondered if David, who was supposed to watch tv with him, was there with them. Would he bother watching tv tonight? He might go to bed early, he had a cold, he thought. He might have a bowl of cornflakes and a cup of milk. He'd love tea and toast.

When he went into his room he didn't switch on the light but sat on his bed looking out on the dimly lit avenue. It was a quiet avenue lined with trees. That was one of the things that appealed to his Mum and to himself. There were no pavs here. At least that was good, he hadn't to be worried coming back late. The houses looked peaceful, brooding, almost asleep!

A car entered the avenue, an Audi, and pulled in the drive-way of the house opposite his. The driver was a blonde lady, who quietly got out and walked slowly. She closed the gate and walked unhurriedly. Suddenly she remembered something and returned sharply. Her high heels pattered. He tried to describe their sound in terms other than pattering.

"She tittups back to the car!"

By now she had entered the house. A bright yellow light flashed on upstairs. He saw her take off her coat. She began to undress, pulling a pullover up and out. He was excited, wrapped in a rug of pleasure. Unfortunately she then drew the curtains. But she continued to undress and he could faintly see her shadow and movements. Then her light went out.

He also went to bed and thought about her. He was surprised that he hadn't seen her before if she lived there. Was she a lodger like himself? Or a rich young lady? Some day he might get a lift from her?

"She tittups and I ululate!" he said.